'There is no such thing as a witch, Idylla, they do not exist, except in the imaginations of those who are too stupid and too uneducated to know better.'

'You are .. sure of .. that?' Idylla asked hesitatingly after a moment.

'Quite sure!' the Marquis answered. 'And I promise you this as well .. I will look after you and protect you. No-one will hurt you ever again.'

Arrow Books by Barbara Cartland

Autobiography

I Search for Rainbows
We Danced All Night

Polly: the Story of My Wonderful Mother
Josephine Empress of France

Romantic Novels

BARBARA CARTLAND

The Blue Eyed Witch

ARROW BOOKS

Arrow Books Limited
3 Fitzroy Square, London W1

An imprint of the Hutchinson Publishing Group

London Melbourne Sydney Auckland
Wellington Johannesburg and agencies
throughout the world

First published by Hutchinson & Co. (Publishers) Ltd., 1976
Arrow edition 1978
© Barbara Cartland 1976

Made and printed in Great Britain
by Cox & Wyman Ltd,
London, Reading and Fakenham

ISBN 0 09 915990 2

Author's Note

Parts of Essex are still known as 'the Witch Country'.

In the last century the whole population, irrespective of social position, were obsessed by a fear of the unknown. Ghosts haunted the fields. The Devil had been known to chase a parson from the pulpit.

In 1860 an old woman in Somerset was accused of afflicting fits upon a child and thrown into a pond with a rope around her middle. In 1924 a smallholder was summonsed for attempting to draw blood from an old woman with a pin and then trying to shoot her. He said she had bewitched his pigs.

Bristol possessed a 'Cunning Woman' as recently as 1930. She was a white witch who discovered lost and stolen property with a needle suspended over a map. Ipswich had a 'Cunning Man' or white wizard who could hypnotise a thief from a distance, so that he wandered round the scene of his crime unable to make his escape.

In 1950 the Witchcraft Act of 1735 was replaced by the Fraudulent Mediums Act. Witchcraft was one of the great tragedies of the human race, consuming thousands in a holocaust of blood and torture. Yet deep in the human mind there still lingers the desire for persecution and the need for a scapegoat.

The details relating to the 'Feast of Venus' at 'The Cloisters' and the Prince of Wales' difficulties with Lady Jersey are factual. As is the huge party given by Mrs Fitzherbert to celebrate her reunion with the Prince in the June of 1800.

1

The Marquis of Aldridge yawned.

If there was one thing that really bored him, he decided, it was a brothel.

In all his relationships with women, which for many years had been the talk of the social world, he had never found his amusement in bawdy houses or paid for the favour of any woman to be found there.

To-night however he had found it difficult not to accept the invitation of his host who was doing his best to entertain the Prince of Wales and rouse him from the despondency in which he had been cast for some weeks.

There was every reason, the Marquis thought, for the Prince to be depressed.

Not only had his marriage proved a disaster, but he was also finding it more difficult than anyone could have imagined to end his liaison with Lady Jersey.

Always emotional, always ready to over-dramatise his feelings, the Prince, because of the violent dislike he had for his wife, Princess Caroline, had decided that the only way he could find solace and comfort was by renewing his love-life with Mrs. Fitzherbert.

As twelve much-advertised nymphs performed out the 'famous Feast of Venus as celebrated in Tahiti', the Marquis was thinking not of them, but of the Prince for whom he had a genuine and deep affection.

He had in fact been a close friend of the Heir to the Throne for the last nine years.

The Marquis was not surprised that Lady Jersey's full-blown charms no longer enthralled the Prince and the sooner he was rid of her the better.

But the lady in question, being extremely determined, was refusing with an obstinacy that was proof against every inducement, to be dislodged from her position as the Royal favourite.

It was, the Marquis thought, principally Lady Jersey who had been responsible for the break-down of the Prince's marriage almost before it had taken place.

Lady Jersey had already attracted him and supplanted Mrs. Fitzherbert in his affections before Princess Caroline had arrived.

Although the bride had been an incredibly bad choice on the part of the King's Ministers, the Royal couple might have had some chance of making their union at least an amicable one, if it had not been for the intervention of Lady Jersey.

"How could he have been such a fool as to like her in the first place?" the Marquis wondered.

And he thought that it was not surprising that from the very beginning Mrs. Fitzherbert had been justifiably jealous.

Lady Jersey had been a serious threat to the Prince's almost idyllic happiness with Mrs. Fitzherbert since the first moment that she had set her cap at the irresponsible, and where women were concerned, extremely susceptible young man.

It was inevitable that she should pursue him, and not only for his position. He was very attractive to look at, witty, amusing, well read, and could, as the Marquis well knew, be a most entertaining companion.

Moreover Lady Jersey herself was an acknowledged beauty, and more than one man had spoken of her "irresistible seduction and fascination".

Even women had said to the Marquis that she was "clever, unprincipled, but beautiful".

The fact that she was nine years older than the Prince and a grandmother was no handicap because he had always liked women older than himself.

The Prince, boyishly impressionable, was captured by her allurements which were exercised with the practised ease of an ambitious, experienced, sensual and heartless woman.

She was in her early forties but he was completely bowled over by her and fervently in love.

"How can he treat me in such a manner?" Mrs. Fitzherbert had wept when she told the Marquis that the Prince had written her a letter under Lady Jersey's direction to say he had "found happiness elsewhere".

"I am afraid, M'am," the Marquis replied, "that Lady Jersey has been persuading His Royal Highness for some time that his connection with you has been unwise. I have heard her say that it is the fact that you are a Roman Catholic which has been the main cause of his unpopularity."

"How can he believe such lies?" Mrs. Fitzherbert gasped.

"She has also averred in my hearing," the Marquis continued, "that the Prince would have had no difficulty in settling his financial affairs satisfactorily had it not been for you!"

Mrs. Fitzherbert was understandably angry.

Both she and the Marquis knew perfectly well that the Prince had spent every penny of the quite considerable fortune she had been left by her late husband.

However, for all Lady Jersey's attractions, the Marquis knew the Prince did not find it easy to live without Mrs. Fitzherbert. In fact he wanted both women at once.

Unfortunately, sweet character thought she was, Mrs. Fitzherbert had a temper and, despite the mediation of the Prince's friends, quarrels over Lady Jersey became continuous.

Finally five years ago, the Prince had severed all connections with Mrs. Fitzherbert and told the King that if he could have his debts paid, he was ready to consider the possibility of being married.

From that moment, the Marquis told himself, everything had gone wrong!

The Prince's friends had hoped that with his marriage he would be free of debt. But as he owed the immense sum of £630,000 this proved impossible.

They also had hoped he would break with Lady Jersey, but he saw more of her than ever and even installed her in a house adjoining Carlton House.

The Marquis was so absorbed in looking back into the past that he suddenly realised that the Feast of Venus had progressed quite a long way since he had even noticed it.

The twelve beautiful nymphs, who were also, everyone had been assured, 'spotless virgins' were giving their performance under the leadership of Queen Oberea, a role taken by Mrs. Hayes herself.

Charlotte Hayes had for some years run the immensely successful establishment of pleasure, which was named 'The Cloisters', in King's Place, Pall Mall.

She was getting older and the Marquis suspected that, having made a large fortune, she would, like her predecessors, soon retire.

She had indeed improved the standard of the notorious 'houses' in London, and looking round at the guests present to-night the Marquis thought it would be difficult to find a more distinguished gathering in any social Salon.

There were twenty-three gentlemen of the nobility present headed by the Prince of Wales, and five other guests were memberes of the House of Commons.

The food was sumptuous, the wine superlative, and although the Marquis was aware they would all have to pay for it eventually there was no doubt that Mrs. Hayes was prepared to give them their money's-worth.

The performing nymphs were certainly very attractive, but the other women present, to whom Mrs. Hayes referred as 'assistant hostesses', were exceedingly experienced in their profession and chosen for their accomplishments as well as their looks.

The Marquis had as a dinner companion, a girl called Yvette who, because it was patriotic to do so, proclaimed herself to be a Belgian, although the Marquis was certain she had been born in France.

She had a nimble wit and a rather fascinating manner of looking at a man from under her eye-lashes.

It was however an old trick with which he was well familiar, and he found it irritating that her small hands with long elegant fingers frequently caressed him.

"You are very silent, M'Lord," Yvette said pouting her red lips provocatively.

It might have excited a younger man, but merely made the Marquis wish to yawn again.

"I find all sorts of charades extremely tiresome," he replied.

Yvette drew a little nearer to him.

"*Vous venez* somewhere quiet *avec moi, mon cher?*" she asked. "I amuse better – much better – than 'charades'. Supper *finit tout de suite*."

The Tahitian Festival, which had been designed, the Marquis realised, from a description given by Hawkesworth, a companion of Captain Cook, in his book, *An Account of a Voyage Round the World (1773)* was practically at an end.

The guests, who had eaten too much and certainly imbibed freely, were now, as they half-lay on the couches which had played an important part in the Festival, abandoning themselves to the enjoyment either of their supper-companions or of the scantily clothed nymphs.

The Prince, the Marquis noted, was exceedingly 'foxed' and had for the moment undoubtedly forgotten his troubles.

But in the morning they would all be back to confront him.

The most difficult problem of all was that Lady Jersey followed him wherever he went and was determined to talk to him even when he did not wish to speak to her.

"One good thing about this evening is that she cannot follow him here," the Marquis told himself.

Then he thought with a feeling of anger that he was almost in the same position as the Prince where Lady Brampton was concerned.

"Why do women never realise when an affair is finished?" he asked himself savagely.

"*Vous dites*, something, M'Lord?' Yvette enquired and he realised he had been expressing his thoughts out loud.

She drew even nearer to him as she spoke and now

her red lips were not far from his as she whispered:

"We amuse ourselves, *Mon brave*? You forget *tout le monde* but Yvette. I make you very happy, *oui*?"

The Marquis put aside her clinging arms and rose to his feet.

"I regret that I suddenly feel unaccountably indisposed," he said. "Please make my apologies to Mrs. Hayes and congratulate her on providing an unusual and extremely colourful entertainment."

"*Non, non, M'Lord!*" Yvette protested.

She was however silenced as the Marquis put a banknote of so high a denomination into her hand that the words she was about to say died in her throat.

Quickly, so that no-one would attempt to stop him, the Marquis left the room and had passed through the outer hall and into King's Place before anyone else at the supper-party was aware of his departure.

His carriage was waiting for him and he threw himself back on the comfortable padded seat. A footman wearing the Aldridge livery placed a light rug over his knees and waited for instructions.

"Home!" the Marquis said briefly.

The door was shut and the horses set off, climbing the steep incline of St. James's into Piccadilly and down Berkeley Street into Berkeley Square.

Aldridge House, magnificent outside and even more breath-taking inside, had been altered and improved by the Marquis's father, who enjoyed building, until it almost rivalled Carlton House in size and luxury.

The Aldridges had always been connoisseurs, and the treasures they had accumulated over the centuries comprised a magnificent collection that was equalled by few other great families in England.

The Marquis, walking across the marble Hall, was

conscious only of his own boredom and had at the moment no appreciation of his surroundings.

He went into the long library whose windows looked out onto the garden at the back of the house and where he habitually sat when he was not entertaining.

The Butler, who had opened the door for him, waited until he was half-way across the room before he said respectfully:

"There's a note on Your Grace's desk. The groom who brought it asked me to say it was urgent."

The Marquis did not reply. He looked towards the note and one glance at the hand-writing told him who it was from.

"Damn the woman!" he said to himself. "Why can she not leave me alone?"

He made no attempt to pick up the note. Instead he sat down in an arm-chair and absent-mindedly accepted the glass of brandy the Butler poured out for him. Then quietly, without speaking, the servant left the room.

The Marquis stared unseeingly at the magnificent picture painted by Rubens which hung on the wall opposite him.

There were few other pictures in the room as the walls were mostly covered with books.

However the glowing colours, exquisite flesh tints, and the allegorical subject made no impression on him.

He was thinking instead of Nadine Brampton's fair beauty and of the determination in her blue eyes which told him she was of the same mould as Lady Jersey. It would not be easy to be rid of her.

Young in years, for she had not yet reached her twenty-sixth birthday, Lady Brampton had the age-old wisdom of Eve, and the Adam she was determined to keep in her very special Garden of Eden was, as the Marquis knew, himself!

Married when she was seventeen to a man much older than she was and who rapidly degenerated into an invalid, Lady Brampton had taken London by storm.

She was beautiful! She was well-bred! She was wealthy!

What was more, her Dresden-china looks disguised a fiery temperament which made her take and discard one lover after another, as in turn she quickly tired of them.

That was until she met the Marquis. Then what should have been an amusing 'affair' and an entertaining interlude became, as far as Lady Brampton was concerned, an *affaire du coeur* in which her heart was completely and irrevocably captured.

The Marquis felt as if he had unexpectedly been caught in a whirlpool of such overwhelming strength that it was dangerous.

Nadine Brampton pursued him until even he, who never put himself out for anyone, and rejoiced in his reputation of being egotistical and supremely selfish, found it hard not to be overwhelmed by her persistence.

If the Prince was troubled by Lady Jersey, he was certainly bedevilled by Lady Brampton to the point when for the first time he was not certain how to end a liaison which had grown both tedious and exasperating.

Lady Brampton bombarded him with notes, presents and invitations.

She called at his house at unpredictable hours, ignoring the fact that she jeopardised what little remained of her reputation in so doing.

She contrived, by some method of her own, to be

at every party, every entertainment, every theatre at which the Marquis was present.

If he rode in the park she appeared and rode beside him. When he was in attendance, which was practically every day, on the Prince at Carlton House, it was almost automatic that as soon as he arrived Lady Brampton would be at the door begging for an audience with His Royal Highness.

Because the Prince was good-humoured and liked pretty women, it was difficult for the Marquis to persuade him to send her away.

Only to-night had it been impossible for her to be present, which the Marquis thought again had been the only redeeming feature of the evening.

He doubted if the imitation Tahitian revels would lift the cloud under which the Prince was suffering and he was quite certain that tomorrow he would have to listen to another long recital of complaints about Lady Jersey, and a dramatic exposition of his ever-increasing desire to make it up with Mrs. Fitzherbert.

If the Prince was taking pains to avoid Lady Jersey, Mrs. Fitzherbert was equally determined to avoid him.

She had given up going to Brighton. She had sold the lease of Marble Hill and was in fact living quietly in a small house at Castle Hill, Ealing, where at the moment she refused to consider the possibility of a reconciliation.

"A link once broken can never be re-joined," she had said to the Marquis when to help the Prince he had pleaded with her to listen to what His Royal Highness had to say.

The Marquis had taken with him presents which included a locket containing a miniature of one of His Royal Highness's eyes painted by Richard Cosway, and a bracelet with the words '*Rejoindre ou mourir*'.

Mrs Fitzherbert had accepted the gifts, but she still refused to meet the giver.

"I shall go mad! I shall die if she will not have me!" the Prince declared dramatically. "Oh, my heart! My heart!"

The Prince was in such a state that the Marquis, like many of his other friends, thought he really might become seriously ill. But there was nothing they could do about it.

"Our positions of course are entirely different," the Marquis told himself. "There is no danger of my making myself ill over Nadine Brampton. At the same time I have to take some action where she is concerned. This cannot go on!"

The Marquis's lips tightened as he thought that owing to her persistence there was every likelihood of his becoming a laughing-stock.

He was very aware that in the past he had broken a great number of hearts.

It was inevitable, since he was not only so good-looking but also had a kind of cynical indifference to love which made women pursue him all the more frantically.

They all started the same way, confident that where others of their sex had failed they would be successful.

The mere fact that he looked at them was enough encouragement to make them believe that this time it would be 'different', this time he would fall in love.

But invariably and disconcertingly quickly they found they were mistaken.

The Marquis was generous when it came to presents. His compliments were more polished and certainly more intelligent than those of any of his contemporaries, and he had an exceptional expertise in 'making love', as every lady on whom he bestowed his favours was ready to declare without contradiction.

But that was all!

No-one could storm the inner citadel of the Marquis's heart.

No-one could be sure after a night of love that they had possessed anything except his body or that even his mind had found them as alluring as his lips had averred.

"You are inhuman!" one lovely lady had told him. "Do you think you are a god, condescending to those who dwell below you? Why else should you be so aloof, so out of reach?"

The Marquis had kissed away her anger, but she had known despairingly that when he left her it was quite likely that she would never see him again.

"You know, Oswin," the Marquis's closest friend, Captain George Summers, had said to him, "if you changed your horses as often as you change your women the country would run out of thoroughbreds!"

The Marquis had laughed.

Captain Summers had served with him in the Army, and because they had shared the hardships of war he allowed him a familiarity which he permitted no-one else.

"Women are dispensable," he said. "Which is why, George, I shall never marry!"

"But you will have to!" Captain Summers argued. "My dear Oswin, it is expected of Marquises. They have to produce heirs!"

"I have some delightful and most respectable cousins," the Marquis answered, "all of whom could take my place admirably. Any of them would uphold with ease the dignity of the title!"

"It is nonsensical to make up your mind on such an important subject at your age," Captain Summers said. "At the same time you should be thinking of settling down. You cannot spend the rest of your life mopping up the Royal tears and changing your bed night after night."

"You certainly have a point there," the Marquis said. "I am sick of creeping up creaking stairs and tip-toeing down ill-lighted passages. I shall confine myself to visiting the very agreeable house I have purchased in Chelsea which is most appropriately near Chelsea Hospital, founded by Nell Gwyn."

"Do you fancy yourself as another Charles II?" Captain Summers asked with a grin.

Then he exclaimed:

"You are not unlike him as a matter of fact! Charles, from all accounts, always monopolised the prettiest women at Court and a new face without fail, distracted his attention from a familiar one."

"He became deeply embroiled with Barbara Castlemaine!" the Marquis retorted.

Captain Summers looked at his friend knowingly.

"Lady Brampton is talking big," he said. "Are you aware that His Lordship is dying? It is doubtful if he will live another two months. Then, Oswin, she will walk you down the aisle."

"She will do nothing of the sort!" the Marquis retorted savagely. "I have told you, George, I have no intention of getting married, and certainly not to Nadine Brampton!"

"She would look spectacular in the Aldridge tiaras," Captain Summers remarked.

"She might do that," the Marquis agreed.

But as he spoke he thought with a kind of horror of

Lady Brampton's possessive hands fastening themselves claw-like round his back.

He had never imagined a woman could be so persistent about what he was determined should be unobtainable.

"Curse it, George! I shall have to go away! I have a damned good mind to join my Regiment again, and fight against Bonaparte."

"There would be no welcome for you there," George Summers said.

"Why the devil not?" the Marquis enquired. "I was a good soldier, as you well know."

"I am not denying that," his friend replied, "but they do not want Marquises in the field, and I cannot imagine you doing nothing but marching up and down Wellington Barracks."

The Marquis did not answer and Captain Summers went on:

"If you should be taken prisoner, you would be too important a feather in Bonaparte's cap for him not to make a victory out of it. I assure you, Oswin, if you rejoin you would not be sent overseas!"

Sitting in his arm-chair now, the Marquis remembered the conversation and knew that his friend, George Summers, had not been talking idly.

At the same time he had spoken the truth when he had said it was impossible for him to stay in London indefinitely playing nursemaid to the Prince and scheming to avoid Lady Brampton.

He was quite certain that tomorrow he would find himself listening all over again to the Prince's lamentations, and undoubtedly like the rest of His Royal Highness's friends, carrying hysterical messages to Ealing.

When he was not doing that there would be Lady Brampton waiting for him, finding out at what time he would be riding, discovering where he would be dining, and if she could not do that, knocking at his door in Berkeley Square.

"I am going to the country," the Marquis decided.

He rose to his feet ready to tug at the bell-pull to summon the Butler. Then he paused.

If he went to Aldridge House in Hertfordshire there was every likelihood that Nadine Brampton would follow him.

She had done that before, arriving when he had chosen a small house-party with care and making it almost impossible for him to turn her away without causing a scene which would reverberate throughout the *Beau Monde*.

He had the feeling that at the moment she would welcome a scandal.

She wanted people to talk about them and he was shrewd enough to realise that by that means she thought she would be able to force him, once she was a widow, to restore her damaged reputation by offering her the protection of his name.

"Blast it! I am like a fox who cannot even run for cover!" the Marquis said.

Then he had an idea.

The day before, his secretary and general factotum, Mr. Graham, had brought him a letter from one of his agents in the country.

Because the Marquis had so many properties he had agents in charge of each one who sent detailed reports of their activities every month, to Mr. Graham at Berkeley Square.

The Marquis's secretary did not trouble him with

these unless they required his personal instructions on a problem that was beyond his jurisdiction.

A recent report from Ridge Castle had been a case in point, and Mr. Graham had drawn his attention to a paragraph in the report which read :

'There has been a lot of local unrest amongst the farm-workers since Sir Harold Trydell died, Sir Caspar, who has inherited the Trydell Estates, is making many local difficulties, changing traditions in a manner which is deeply resented not only by the farmers, but also by the labourers themselves.

I have the feeling, perhaps unfounded, that if things go on as they are, we may have riots on our hands. I hope I am mistaken, but I would like His Lordship's authority to do what I can to soothe the rising feelings of resentment perhaps by employing more of the local men ourselves and thus alleviating distress.'

"Sir Harold is dead then !" the Marquis had exclaimed when he handed the report back to Mr. Graham.

"He died three months ago, My Lord. I did tell you at the time, but perhaps you did not hear me."

"It certainly comes as a surprise to me now," the Marquis said. "I never cared for Caspar Trydell. It is a pity his elder brother was drowned."

"It was indeed, My Lord," Mr. Graham said. "You knew Mr. John, I believe."

"We were friends when he was a boy and lived at the Castle," the Marquis replied.

"Yes, of course, My Lord."

"He could have managed the Estates well, but he never had a chance. Sir Harold was a very bigoted old

22

man and a tyrant where his sons were concerned," the Marquis remarked.

"It seems as if Sir Caspar has inherited some of his father's peculiarities."

"I am sure of that," the Marquis said reflectively. "I have seen Caspar Trydell sometimes in London, although he moves in a very different set of people from my circle. He has always seemed to be something of a Rake – perhaps that is not the right word – débauché would be more appropriate."

He paused as if he was thinking. Then he said:

"I remember John Trydell telling me that his brother was always in debt. But I should imagine Sir Harold was warm in the pocket when he died, and his only surviving son will have inherited everything he possessed."

"That is true," Mr. Graham agreed, "although it will be troublesome, My Lord, if he upsets the local people. They are different in Essex from other counties. It is an isolated part of the country and to me the peasants seem still almost mediaeval in their outlook."

The Marquis had thought that Mr. Graham was exaggerating, but now he remembered the conversation and it gave him an idea.

He would visit Ridge Castle. He had not been there for several years; in fact he very seldom thought of his Estate perched on the promontory that was bordered on one side by the Blackwater River and on the other by the sea.

Wild and desolate, he had loved it as a boy and had spent most of his holidays there because his father found children troublesome.

"I will go to the Castle," he decided. "I will tell Graham that no-one, no-one in London, must know where I have gone. That will cover my tracks as far as

Nadine Brampton is concerned, and I will write a personal note of explanation to the Prince."

He was so pleased at the idea of escaping in this way, that the boredom which had encompassed him all the evening lifted a little.

He even thought he might visit the delectable actress he had recently installed in the house he had described to George Summers as being near Chelsea Hospital.

There was something about Hester Delfine that reminded him vaguely of Nell Gwyn.

She was better educated and certainly a better actress. She had a sharp wit which amused the Marquis and she was not unlike Charles's 'pretty Nelly' in that she had red hair.

He had never been particularly enamoured of redheaded women, preferring them to be blonde with blue eyes.

"It is because you are dark, darling," Lady Brampton had told him in a moment of intimacy when he was measuring the length of her long golden hair as she lay beside him.

"Must one always do the expected?" the Marquis had asked with a note of irritation in his voice.

"Why not?" Nadine Brampton had enquired. "Dark men like fair women, and if they are tall and big they like them small and petite; while short men invariably run after a Juno or an Amazon, just as small dogs run after big ones."

It was perhaps this more than anything else that had made the Marquis choose a new mistress with red hair.

It was expected that gentlemen of fashion should set up a mistress with a house and a carriage, and the fact that Hester Delfine was fervently admired by the

24

Bucks of St. James's might also have had something to do with the Marquis's choice.

It had amused him to sweep her off from under their very noses, and he decided now that, while he had told her it would be too late for him to come and see her that evening after Mrs. Hayes's Festival, he would change his mind.

He rang the bell and when the Butler answered within a few seconds he said :

"Order a carriage and inform Mr. Graham that I am leaving first thing in the morning for the country."

"Yes, My Lord, and will you be staying long?"

"I have no idea," the Marquis replied. "I shall leave at nine o'clock."

This meant, the Butler knew, that His Lordship's valets, who had retired to bed, must be aroused immediately to start packing.

It also meant that His Lordship would travel as usual with not only his Phaeton but also a travelling chariot carrying his valets and his luggage, six outriders, and his favourite horse, with a special groom in charge.

It was an expedition which naturally required a great deal of planning, and that this would not have to be done at a moment's notice meant that most of the household in Berkeley Square would be up all night.

That he might have caused any inconvenience to his staff never crossed the Marquis's mind.

It was what they were paid for, and he expected everything to be perfectly organised and his instructions carried out without a hitch, however short notice was given.

It said a great deal for the organisation in the stables that a carriage was at the door in less than five minutes.

When the Marquis gave the address in Chelsea to the Butler, he passed it to the footman on the box of the carriage who passed it to the coachman.

There was no note or intonation in the voices of any of the flunkeys to indicate that they had any idea of where the Marquis was going, and yet they all knew.

There was a faint smile on the Butler's face as he walked back into the lighted Hall of Aldridge House to give the orders to set in motion the elaborate machinery which must start rolling immediately if the Marquis was to leave at the appointed time tomorrow morning.

"His Lordship's a real chip off the old block!" he told himself, and now there was no doubt of the smile on his lips.

There was not a man in the whole household who was not secretly rather proud of the fact that their master was something of a Rake. It was in the Aldridge tradition.

The Marquis travelled to Chelsea with a speed that he expected from the horses on which he expended large sums of money.

He drew up outside the house in Royal Avenue, a pleasant situation where there were shady trees and a degree of privacy which the Marquis found agreeable.

The footman stepped down to ring the bell, and it was some minutes before the door was opened by a surprised-looking maid, her cap crooked on her head, her apron hastily tied.

"His Lordship!" the footman said.

"We wasn't expecting 'im ter-night!"

"Well, 'e's, 'ere now, ain't 'e?" the footman remarked under his breath so that the Marquis would not hear their exchange.

He walked back to open the door of the carriage and the Marquis stepped out languidly.

He had already begun to regret his impetuosity in deciding to call on Hester when he might have retired to bed.

At the same time, as he was going away, it would be only fair to inform her he would be absent. Otherwise undoubtedly, like Lady Brampton, she would worry about him.

He entered the small, narrow hall of the house and noticed with distaste there was a pungent smell of cooking.

"Madame 'asn't been back from the theatre long, M'Lord!" the maid said. "She's in the Dining-Room."

This was a small room at the back of the house which the Marquis found somewhat uninviting and seldom entered.

Whenever he gave Hester supper it was invariably at one of the gay places in the West End that catered for the theatrical profession.

Or else they attended one of the innumerable parties given by the 'gay sparks' who found it amusing to entertain the ladies who were endowed with the glamour of the footlights.

Now the Marquis crossed the hall and the maid opened the door of the Dining-Room.

Hester was seated at the table and with her was a well-known actor whom the Marquis had met in her company on several occasions.

Their heads were close together as he entered and he had the unavoidable impression that he was intruding.

They looked up in astonishment and Hester gave a little cry.

"My Lord! I had no idea you would be visiting me this evening!"

"I had no idea myself!" the Marquis replied. "I came on an impulse, having found the party at 'The Cloister' incredibly boring!"

"I warned you it would be!" Hester Delfine said.

She had risen to her feet and the man beside her had risen too.

The Marquis nodded to him coldly.

"Good evening, Merridon!"

"Hester was feeling lonely, My Lord, and she asked me to join her. I hope you have no objection?"

"Why should I?" the Marquis replied.

"You will have some wine, My Lord?" Hester asked.

As she spoke she drew another chair up to the small round table in the centre of the room.

As the Marquis had supplied the wine they were both drinking, he felt slightly annoyed that they had chosen the most expensive champagne of which he had only a limited supply.

It had perhaps been foolhardy of him to have sent two cases to the house in Chelsea.

But he had thought that when he visited Hester there would be no better occasion to indulge in a wine which was getting more expensive and more difficult to procure from France as hostilities raged across the Channel.

There was however only a little left in the bottle and Hester signalled to the footman, who had appeared in the Dining-Room since the Marquis's entrance, to open another.

With difficulty the Marquis prevented himself from suggesting an inferior wine.

"Will you have something to eat?" Hester asked, smiling at him ingratiatingly.

The Marquis shook his head.

"I have already been regaled with a gigantic banquet prepared presumably with Tahiti in mind, but which was undoubtedly French and English with the predominance unfortunately on the British side!"

The actor laughed.

"And what was the performance like, My Lord?"

"Somewhat amateurish," he replied, "but what can you expect from virgins?"

"If they were!" Hester said sarcastically. "I would not trust Charlotte Hayes an inch! She is obviously trying to vie with Mrs. Fawkland who has opened Temples of Aurora, Flora and Mystery."

"I have not sampled such exotic delights," Mr. Merridon remarked, "but Mr. Sheridan told me that the Temple of Flora was quite amusing."

"That is where she keeps the older, well-trained and more experienced girls," Hester explained.

The Marquis looked bored.

He had heard his friends in White's extolling the virtues of the latest brothel which at least had some semblance of imagination about it.

The Temple of Aurora offered very young girls. The Temple of Flora those that were older, and Mystery was supposed to be exotic, or what the Marquis thought of as unpleasantly debauched.

It was a place that would never interest him. But now, because he was thinking of visiting Ridge Castle, he remembered that someone in the Club had told him that Caspar Trydell was an habitué of the Temple of Mystery.

As he sipped his champagne, he was aware that the Dining-Room smelt even more pungently unpleasant than the hall.

He looked at what Hester and her companion were eating and realised it was pigs' trotters, a dish for which he had always had an aversion.

As if she realised what he was thinking Hester said:

"Forgive me, My Lord, if my choice of menu offends you, but Frank and I found it was a taste we had in common, just as we both like eel soup, with which we started our supper."

This was another dish for which the Marquis had a disgust.

He had seen the eels all too often after they had been caught in the Thames and were for sale on the winkle-stalls along the Embankment and down by the docks.

They reminded him of snakes, of which he had been frightened as a child when an adder had bitten a game-keeper with whom he was out shooting.

He had never forgotten the man's consternation which later had turned to agony, and for a week his life had hung by a thread.

Snakes and eels were connected in his mind with everything which was unpleasant and to be avoided. He decided suddenly that he had no wish to stay any longer with Hester.

Frank Merridon had already realised this was his cue to leave, and hastily finishing his glass of champagne he rose to his feet.

"I must be getting off home," he said. "I have an early rehearsal tomorrow."

Hester gave him an apologetic glance.

He was important in the theatre and she did not wish to offend him. At the same time it was quite obvious that he was *de trop* once the Marquis had appeared.

The Marquis too had risen.

"I also have an early start in the morning," he said, "and so I beg you to finish your supper and I will leave you in peace to do so."

"No, no! You must not go!" Hester said quickly.

The Marquis walked towards the door and she followed him putting her hand on his arm to look up at him.

"Please stay," she pleaded.

"I merely came to tell you, Hester, that I have to leave London early tomorrow morning," the Marquis said. "I may not be back for a week or so."

"You are going away? This is very unexpected!"

"I have some important business to attend to on one of my properties," the Marquis said. "Forgive me for interrupting such a delightful supper-party. It was inconsiderate of me, but I hope you understand."

He raised her hand to his lips as he spoke, and those who knew the Marquis well could have warned Hester that when he was at his most polite he was also at his most dangerous.

He walked down the narrow hall and she fluttered after him.

"Can you not stay just for a little while?" she asked when they were out of ear-shot of the Dining-Room. "I want you, as you well know! I want you to be with me!"

"Another time," the Marquis said firmly.

As he opened the front door the warm night air was a relief from the odour of pork.

He drew in his breath.

"Good-bye, Hester!" he said and walked across the pavement to his carriage.

She did not realise as she waved to him that it was indeed good-bye!

2

The Marquis set off from Berkeley Square the following morning in a good humour.

He had slept well. It did not concern him that most of the members of his household had been up all night.

The Coachman in particular had sent ahead a team in charge of four grooms at the first light of dawn so that they would be ready for the Marquis to change horses at Chelmsford.

He ate a large breakfast, not drinking, as so many of his contemporaries did, brandy or beer, but coffee.

Coffee had become very popular in London and new coffee-shops were continually opening to supply the demand for it.

It was also superseding tea as the fashionable drink among the Ladies of Quality which made many of the older men stick to their contention that ale or brandy was the proper drink for a gentleman first thing in the morning.

The Marquis however had always been concerned with keeping himself athletically fit.

He fenced at least three or four times a week with the masters of the art, he boxed at 'Gentleman Jackson's Rooms' in Piccadilly and the abnormal amount of riding he also did kept his body so strong that he was the despair of his tailors.

While he was undoubtedly one of the smartest and

best-dressed of the Bucks who surrounded the Prince of Wales – in fact Beau Brummell had often quoted him as an example – only his tailor knew how difficult it was to dress with close-fitting elegance a body which rippled with muscles.

It was fashionable to appear languid and clothes must, according to Brummell's edicts, fit to perfection without appearing conspicuous.

That the Marquis achieved this to a notable degree was due to the fact that, while he wished all the accoutrements to be as near perfect as possible, his mind was concerned with a great many more important things than his personal appearance.

Nevertheless as he stepped out of Aldridge House it would have been difficult to imagine that a man could look smarter, more handsome and indeed more irresistibly attractive.

Below the white breeches and cut-away coat his hessians polished with champagne reflected the phaeton, and his cravat was tied in one of the difficult and complicated patterns which was the despair of most Dandies.

The Marquis set his hat slightly on one side of his dark head and picked up the reins.

"Good-bye, Graham," he said to his secretary. "Do not fail to carry out my instructions."

"They will be put into operation immediately, My Lord!" Mr. Graham replied with just a note of rebuke in his voice.

The Marquis was well aware that his Secretary had an utterly reliable memory which was instrumental in keeping the whole machinery of Aldridge House and his other properties working smoothly with seldom a hitch.

He was however referring to his instructions to Mr. Graham to have a note containing a large cheque carried to Hester Delfine in Chelsea and to make sure she vacated the property as soon as possible.

The Marquis was not a vindictive man and, although he suspected Hester would spend the night in Frank Merridon's arms, that was not the real reason why he wished to be rid of her.

It was partly, he admitted to himself, the smell of pork which he disliked and partly that the two of them, sitting in his Dining-Room drinking his wine, had seemed to be guzzling their food in a somewhat vulgar manner.

To him the whole scene had seemed degradingly coarse.

It was too reminiscent of a Restoration drama. The favourite mistress entertaining the man of her choice, the arrival of the rich protector, the almost over-controlled manner in which they faced the situation, all made the Marquis remember the evening with a sense of disgust.

He had told himself often enough that he was over-fastidious.

But just as his own surroundings were redolent with good taste and ornamented with precious treasures to delight the eye of a connoisseur, so he expected all other details in his life to conform to the same pattern.

His mistresses were always beautiful, intelligent, with certain qualities which were out of the ordinary.

Similarly in his love-affairs with members of the *Beau Monde* he sought out those who were described as 'Incomparables' and were acknowledged Queens of their own set.

But Hester last night had proclaimed all too obviously

that her humble origin and commonplace tastes were very different from the impression she created behind the footlights.

There she had an aura and a glamour about her which had made the Marquis seek her out in the first place, and her acting ability had made him on closer acquaintance overlook many blemishes which, he told himself now, might have cooled his interest sooner.

Nevertheless, as he had informed Mr. Graham, the affair was finished.

He had been generous, as he always was, in writing the cheque which had accompanied his letter of farewell.

He had also most politely thanked her for the pleasure she had given him, but he had known as he signed his name that it was for the last time.

As he drove away he felt he was also escaping skilfully from Lady Brampton.

He had not opened the note she had sent him last night, but instead he had instructed Mr. Graham to return it to her with the information that 'His Lordship had left London for an indefinite period.'

It would give Nadine Brampton food for thought, but he was quite certain she would not find him at Ridge Castle.

With his passion for detail he had made it clear to Mr. Graham that the whole household was to be instructed that, however closely they were questioned, none of them, from the Butler to the lowest pantry-boy, had the slightest idea where he might be.

Those who served at Aldridge House knew when they were engaged that to give away information of any sort about their master was to make certain of instant dismissal without a reference.

At the same time the Marquis was well aware how skilful Nadine Brampton and other women like her could be when they wanted information.

He had known in the past of very large bribes which his servants had been offered, of occasions when they had been taken to an Inn and plied with drink to make them talk more freely, and others when they had actually been threatened unless they disclosed certain details of his itinerary.

"You will be quite safe from interruption, My Lord," Mr. Graham had told him. "Only the stable and the pantry will be aware of your destination, and you can trust Rigby to control the stable-lads and Bowden the footmen."

"If there is anything really urgent," the Marquis said, "you can send me a message by a groom, but otherwise deal with everything yourself. I have already written to His Royal Highness telling him that I have been called to the country on urgent family matters. That will keep him quiet for a little while at any rate."

"His Royal Highness will miss you, My Lord," Mr. Graham said respectfully.

"He has plenty of people to take my place," the Marquis replied lightly.

He thought that George had been right; he certainly should not spend any more time mopping up the Royal tears.

As the Marquis tooled his horses through the traffic of the city with a skill which made a great many people turn to watch him pass, he thought that for the first time for months he felt free as a school-boy starting off on his holiday.

Although selfish and extremely egotistical where his

own affairs were concerned, nevertheless, the Marquis had a patriotism which no-one who knew him well would deny.

He realised, as few other people seemed to do, that the Prince of Wales's attitude and feeling towards Britain were of the utmost importance to the stability of the country, not only at the moment but also in the future.

If he did not soon inherit the Throne, there was every likelihood of his being appointed Regent before his father's death.

The King was growing more and more unpredictable in his behaviour and there were rumours that he was displaying again all the symptoms that had characterised his serious illness in 1788.

His physical condition had weakened and his conduct became at times what his doctors called 'very extravagant'.

This meant that he became violent to the extent that the number of keepers required for him had to be doubled.

It also meant that it was important for the Prince to take a greater interest in politics.

Thanks to the Marquis's influence he had grown close once more to the Opposition, giving dinners at Carlton House for Charles Fox, Sheridan, the Duke of Norfolk and other leading opponents of the Government.

At one time it had seemed possible, although the Marquis had never really credited it, that a new Government might be formed by some of the Opposition and various disgruntled members of the present Administration, under the auspices of the Prince.

But unfortunately the Prince's wide-spread unpopularity after his marriage had stood immovably in the way.

However the dinner-parties renewed His Royal Highness's partiality to politics, despite the fact that one of the guests remarked cynically :

"At four o'clock in the morning, the Prince's oratorial powers decline with each bottle of wine consumed!"

That might have been true, but another privileged guest said firmly that he had never heard "worse reasoning in better or more brilliant language".

This confirmed the Marquis's own ideas that the Prince had an excellent brain and a quickness of intellect which only needed channelling in the right direction.

'I have certainly done my best,' he thought with a sigh, 'but I am entitled to my "time off" like everyone else.'

The team of four thoroughbred and extremely expensive chestnuts he was driving were soon clear of the London traffic.

Now they were out in the open country driving into Essex which the Marquis had always thought was one of the wildest as well as the most backward of the counties surrounding London.

The reason for this, he felt, might be the fact that in that county there were few great aristocratic landlords, but the land was held by yeoman farmers and Squires, Essex born and bred, who for generations, had seldom travelled outside the boundaries of their own lands.

He had often wondered what had possessed his greatgrandfather to buy Ridge Estate in such an isolated area.

The Castle, although it must always have been attractive, had little to recommend it until his father spent very large sums of money restoring and re-decorating it.

He had done this principally, as far as the Marquis could make out, so that he could send his only son there to be out of the way during, as he had always proclaimed publicly, 'those tiresome and quite unnecessary holidays'.

But to the Marquis the Castle had held an enchantment which compensated for what a less intelligent boy might have found an almost alarming loneliness.

There had been only a number of servants and an elderly Tutor to keep him company.

But he had grown to know the tenant farmers and found at last a kind friend and a hero to worship in John Trydell whose father's estates marched with those of the Castle.

When he was older, the Marquis often wondered what had prompted John Trydell, who was ten years his senior, to show such kindness to a small boy.

The answer he decided lay in the fact that John was also lonely and unhappy at home.

It was John who taught him to shoot, who took him coursing and otter-hunting.

It was John who taught him about the country-side, showed him the badgers' lair, a fox's den, and where the rare birds nested.

In the summer, although the Marquis had never been the brilliant swimmer John was, they had raced each other across the Blackwater River and swum quite alarming distances out to sea.

The Marquis had almost forgotten the enjoyment of those care-free days.

But now the scenery of Essex, the smell of the countryside, the small fields enclosed with high hedge-rows, brought it all back to him.

The bluebells growing in the woods, the blossom on the fruit-trees, the profusion of wild birds caused him to remember it was nesting time.

He drove on, reaching Chelmsford in record time.

The travelling chariot carrying his luggage, his valets and an under-secretary trained by Mr. Graham to take over the smooth running of the Castle while he was in residence, had long been left behind.

Three out-riders escorted the chariot while three others rode just behind, keeping the Marquis within sight but on his instructions well clear of the dust thrown up by the wheels of his phaeton from the narrow roads.

At Chelmsford there was an excellent meal awaiting him in the private parlour of the Coaching Inn.

It had been ordered by Mr. Graham, who had sent a note of instructions by the grooms who had arrived early in the morning with the horses.

These had since been resting in comfortable stables awaiting His Lordship's arrival.

Mr. Graham was well aware that a Posting-Inn could not supply dishes like those prepared for his master by the French Chef at Aldridge House.

Cooking at Inns was usually deplorable, just as in many gentlemen's houses the ingredients despite being fresh and of excellent quality were badly prepared and usually served lukewarm.

All the aristocrats who could afford it employed a French Chef, following the example of His Royal Highness whose Chef at Carlton House was the envy of his guests.

It had been the Marquis who impressed upon the Heir to the Throne that it was not only wine that was important, but also the food that went with it.

Dinners held at Aldridge House were a gastronomic treat and had awoken such a competitive spirit in the Prince that those who habitually accepted his hospitality thanked the Marquis for the vast improvement in food served at Carlton House.

But while the Marquis had an epicurean taste when in London, he was quite prepared when in the country to accept English fare as long as it was the best.

Mr Graham had arranged that that was what he was provided with at 'The Dog and Duck' when he stopped there at midday.

The steak and kidney pie was cooked to a turn, the pastry crisp and brown, and the roast mutton with caper sauce was tender and not over-cooked.

The pigeons had been turning on a spit until the very moment when the Marquis drove into the yard, and there was a ham so well cured by the Inn Keeper's wife that although it had not been on Mr. Graham's menu the Marquis pronounced it excellent!

He drank the local ale and finished his meal with a glass of brandy which after the first sip made him raise his eye-brows.

He was convinced, although he was too tactful to say so, that it had been smuggled.

The Essex marshes had been notorious in the last few years for being a landing place for smugglers. Although it was a shorter passage from France to the south coast of England it was also infinitely more dangerous.

Large boats, especially built for the purpose, found it easy to land unobserved in Essex with a greater amount of cargo and without the anxiety which was attendant on every attempt to land on the south coast under the watchful eye of the coast guards.

The brandy was in fact so good that the Marquis had a second glass. Then knowing that his horses would be ready and waiting for him he strolled into the yard.

He thanked the landlord for his repast and tipped the two rosy-cheeked maids who had waited on him with a munificence that made them speechless with gratitude.

He then climbed back into his phaeton and picking up his reins saw with satisfaction that the team of roans which were now between the shafts were as fine, if not finer, than the chestnuts which he had driven from London.

They were in fact a new acquisition. He had purchased them at Tattersalls from a nobleman who had been forced to part with them after a night of almost insane gaming at Wattiers.

The Marquis gambled occasionally, but he had never had the wild, intemperate compulsion which animated so many personalities of the period.

Charles Fox, for instance, despite his brilliance as a politician, had developed as a young man an insatiable passion for gambling, which was to lead him into being almost constantly in debt throughout the whole of his life.

In his mid-20's he would arrive to speak in the House of Commons after playing 'Hazard' at Almack's for more than twenty-four hours at a stretch.

In three nights he and his brother lost £32,000 between them.

All London laughed at the story that when his father

was informed of a rumour that Charles was to be married, the old man had said:

"I am glad of that; for then he will go to bed for at least one night!"

But whatever the reason for his being able to acquire the horses he was now driving, the Marquis was delighted that they had come into his possession.

They were certainly outstanding, and he decided that next time he went to Newmarket for the races he would drive them there and know with satisfaction that they would be unrivalled by any other team.

The Marquis was now driving along narrow, twisting roads which demanded all his skill.

Once past Danbury and on to Purleigh he reached a road which ran south of the Blackwater River.

Now the Marquis was on familiar ground and he realised that shortly he would reach the boundary of his own estate.

There was however the small village of Steeple which he did not own, and as he neared it he saw to his surprise a large number of people moving along the road ahead of him.

It was unusual at this time of the day, when most of the peasants were working in the fields, to find them congregated in the village.

As he reined in his horses, the thought crossed his mind that perhaps this was one of the disturbances that might develop into a riot about which his agent at the Castle had written to Mr. Graham.

Then he saw the peasants, the men wearing their smocks and the women with shawls over their heads, had something or somebody whom they appeared to be dragging or carrying along with them.

Small boys circling round the outside of the group

43

were shouting and throwing pieces of grass or mud which they picked up from the side of the road.

So intent was the crowd on what they were doing that the Marquis's horses were almost upon them before they realised it.

A few men at the back of the group turned round at the clatter of hooves, shouted to the others, and the crowd moved to the side of the roadway.

It was perhaps the expressions on their faces which made the Marquis certain this was in fact a riot and made him pull his horses to a standstill and ask in a loud, authoritative tone which none of the peasants could fail to hear:

"What is going on here?"

An older man, near to the phaeton, looked a trifle more intelligent than the rest and the Marquis addressed him:

"I am the Marquis of Aldridge," he said, "and I am on my way to Ridge Castle. What has happened? Why are you not working at this time of the day?"

As the Marquis introduced himself the elderly man's finger instinctively went up to his forelock, and before he replied he respectfully took off his battered felt hat.

"We've a witch wi'us, M'Lord!" he said. "And us be atakin' 'er for a duckin'!"

"A witch?" the Marquis exclaimed in surprise. "How do you know she is a witch?"

Even as he spoke he remembered that Essex was a notoriously superstitious county and had a history of witchcraft and suppression of witches that dated back to Elizabethan times.

"Us found 'er on th' Druid stones, M'Lord," the man answered. " 'er be lyin' there asleep after makin' a sac-

44

rifice. The cock were with 'er – one o' Bel Malden's it be – an' blood all over 'er gown!''

The Marquis threw the reins to his groom and stepped down from the phaeton.

"I will see for myself."

He was certain as he spoke that this was no witch, but some miserable old woman, perhaps wandering in her mind and a trifle senile. She would have incurred the enmity of the village simply because she lived alone and they were frightened of her.

The Marquis's tall, commanding presence made the villagers who had been silent since he had drawn up his phaeton open the way for him to where they had laid the witch down on the ground.

From their rough treatment of her and the mud and rubbish that had been thrown, her body, which was covered in what had been a dark cloak, looked singularly unpleasant.

In fact at first sight the Marquis thought that in all probability the woman was already dead.

The ducking of witches was, he knew, a mediaeval and extremely cruel test.

With a rope round the woman's waist, and usually stripped of most of her clothes, the supposed witch was flung into a pond in the belief that if she sank she was innocent and if she floated she was guilty.

If the witch sank, as was to be expected, she was dragged back to the bank, tested again and again until usually she was drowned.

The woman lying on the grass had, the Marquis saw, long dark hair which might suggest supernatural powers, but it certainly did not look as if it belonged to anyone elderly.

It had soft lights in it. Then he noticed that on the

top of her head there was a patch red with blood, as if she had been hit violently with a weapon of some sort.

"You have certainly handled this woman roughly!" he said accusingly to the elderly man who had followed him to the witch's side.

"Us didn't do that, M'Lord," the old man protested. "She's th' way us found 'er, 'cept the women scratched 'er to see if 'er'd bleed."

This the Marquis knew was another test, for a witch was supposed to have special parts of her body which would not bleed even if she were pricked with a needle.

It was usual for her to be scratched on her face and arms by those who dragged her in front of a judge.

"There were blood on 'er gown from th' cock," the old man said as if he was anxious to convince the Marquis they were justified in what they had done.

There was no doubt, however, that the peasants were now somewhat apprehensive.

They well knew they had no right to take the law into their own hands; if they suspected a woman of being a witch, she should have been taken in front of a Magistrate to be sent for trial.

Essex was proud of the fact that the first major trial of witches had taken place at Chelmsford in 1556, and there had been numerous instances all down the centuries in which Essex witches had been brought to trial on monstrous allegations of witchcraft and sorcery.

"Let me look at her," the Marquis ordered.

The elderly man bent down, turned the woman on her back and swept away the long dark hair which had fallen forward to cover her face.

The Marquis could see at once that this was no old woman but a very young one.

Her face had been scratched so that there was blood on her cheeks and on her forehead. But despite it he was able to see the perfection of her features and the fact that the skin on her face where it was not bloodstained was extremely white.

It was doubtful, he thought, if she was more than eighteen. There was something delicate and refined about her small straight nose and winged eye-brows, while her little pointed face made it somehow impossible to think of her being connected with evil.

"Look at th' blood – th' blood, M'Lord!" the old man said pointing to her skirt.

She wore a gown which the Marquis realised proclaimed her to be of a very different class to her persecutors.

There was a muslin fichu, now torn and dirtied by rough hands, which had encircled the whiteness of her neck, and there was a large patch of blood, doubtless from the dead cock, in the centre of her full skirts.

"She was on the Druid stones?" the Marquis asked.

"Aye, M'Lord, young Rod found 'er when 'e were passing on 'is way to work. 'e called t'others and they sees 'er were a witch. No-one but a witch, M'Lord, would lie on th' Druid stones at night!"

The Marquis knew this was true.

There were many superstitions repeated and re-repeated about the huge stones which stood on a bare piece of ground overlooking the river.

He himself had always believed they were more likely to have been placed there by the Vikings as a land-mark.

But for the local peasantry it was a place of sacrificial magic which had been there since the times of the

47

Druids, and they would no more venture by the stones at night than spend the hours of darkness in a graveyard!

"She was lying there unconscious as she is now?" the Marquis enquired.

As he spoke he noted that the witch's eye-lashes were very long and dark against the almost translucent clarity of her skin.

" 'er be a-sleeping, M'Lord, after a sacrificial orgy," a voice said from the crowd.

It was a woman's voice and the Marquis heard the venom in it.

He remembered that women were always more virulent and more cruel in their persecution of witches than any man.

It was the women, he thought looking down, who had inflicted the criss-cross scratches on the girl's cheeks and on her arms; some were so deep they had torn away the flesh.

And it would have been the women who had clutched at the muslin fichu round her neck and perhaps incited the boys to bespatter her gown and cloak with mud and filth.

He looked again at the great patch of blood, then said:

"Are you suggesting that this witch, if she is one, sacrificed the cock herself?"

"That 'er did, M'Lord!" said another woman from the crowd. "Wrang its neck an' drank its blood, no doubt. Blood to give 'er power to fly to th' Devil!"

"Whatever the killing was for," the Marquis said, "I asked you a question. Are you saying that she killed the cock herself?"

"Aye, that's what we says."

"That's what 'er did!"

More than one voice was speaking now and some-body came forward to throw the cock down at the Marquis's feet.

"There it be, M'Lord! As ye can see its neck's been atwisted so 'ard 'tis broken off!"

It had been quite a fine young cock, the Marquis noticed. It would have required considerable strength to have twisted the head almost clear of its body.

It looked an unpleasant mess now with its broken neck and bloodstained feathers. He glanced at it for a moment. Then he said in a quiet voice that commanded attention:

"If that is true, will one of you tell me why there is no blood on the witch's hands?"

Everyone present moved forward, craning their necks to stare at the girl's hands which lay limp and motionless on either side of her body.

They were small hands, white and soft with long thin, sensitive fingers and almond-shaped nails.

While everything else about her was bloody from scratches or dirty from mud, her hands were un-blemished.

As the peasants stared there was only silence.

"Those of you who kill your own cockerels for the pot," the Marquis said, "are well aware that it re-quires considerable strength to twist a bird's neck. It would be impossible to do so in the manner in which this cock has been treated without getting blood upon one's hands."

"Perhaps 'er magicked it off?" someone suggested, but the voice was uncertain.

"Let we put it to th' test, M'Lord," the elderly man said. "If 'er sinks, 'er'll be innocent right enough."

"You have no right to test a witch unless she has been brought to trial," the Marquis answered. "You know that as well as I do, and I expect when this girl regains consciousness she will be able to give a reasonable explanation as to why she should have been left on the Druid stones. And why, unless someone intended her to be persecuted, she should have a dead cock beside her."

The Marquis looked reprovingly around him and now the peasants were somewhat shame-faced.

"Us were only a-doing wot us thought be right, M'Lord, an' there's several people round 'ere as thinks they've been inflicted with th' 'evil eye'."

"Aye, that's true right enough!" a chorus averred.

"Will Halstead lost a cow las' week. Well 'er be in th' morn, dead as a door-nail by dusk!"

"That is not evidence that it was the work of this woman," the Marquis said sternly. "Go back to your work, and another time remember the Magistrates are there to pass judgement, not you."

His tone was severe and the peasants on the outside of the crowd began to move away sheepishly.

The fire had gone out of them, and now it was difficult to understand why the slight, limp figure lying on the ground had aroused so much hatred, fear and animosity.

"What'll us do with 'er, M'Lord?" the elderly man asked. "It be a long way t'Chelmsford. Oi doubts if anyone'll carry 'er in their cart."

The Marquis considered for a moment, then said:

"I will take her in my phaeton."

"You'll take 'er, M'Lord?"

"I will try to find out the truth about her," the Marquis said. "I doubt if she is alive, and as you have handled her so roughly you may all find yourselves charged with murder!"

A shiver of apprehension ran through the rest of the bystanders, and now they turned and moved away so swiftly it was almost as if they vanished.

Only the old man and a vacant-looking youth were left, the lad still holding a handful of mud in his hand.

"Pick her up!" the Marquis commanded, "and lay her on the floor of the phaeton!"

The two men did as they were told.

It was not hard to lift the unconscious girl. She obviously weighed little and they laid her down on the floor of the Marquis's phaeton and pulled her dirt-stained cloak over her body so that only her face and hair were uncovered.

The Marquis got into the driving-seat and thought as he did so that his groom relinquished the reins rather more quickly than was usual and hurriedly climbed on to his seat at the back.

The Marquis brought his long whip down lightly on the horses' backs and they started forward.

He did not speak to the old man again, and as he drove on he found the street was empty. There were only a few ducks swimming on the pond in the centre of the village-green where the witch would have been ducked.

It was only another six miles to the Castle, and almost immediately on leaving the village the Marquis was on his own land.

He saw with satisfaction that the fields which had been well ploughed were sown with wheat and barley.

There was a smell of salt on the warm air and there was too the fragrance of wild flowers.

The gulls were swirling overhead and the Marquis noted a large family of young partridges which ran across the road to safety just before the horses reached them.

It was wild and empty, flat and yet somehow exhilarating as it had been when he was a boy.

When he saw the Castle standing silhouetted against the blue of the sky he felt a sudden elation within himself that was very unlike his usual cynical and bored attitude to everything.

Grey and formidable, the tower was Norman and looked as if it was ready to repel any invader.

The rest of the house, which had been added later, had the fine architectural and classical lines that William Adam — the Scottish architect — portrayed so brilliantly.

He had made Ridge Castle exceedingly beautiful by incorporating the great Norman tower so that it blended with the new building without seeming in the least alien to it.

The trees that surrounded the Castle protected it from the violence of the winter storms and now enclosed it with a soft green which seemed like emerald velvet.

At the front there was a profusion of golden daffodils looking like a carpet of glory, and the Marquis felt that they trumpeted his arrival and made him welcome.

He drew up with a flourish in front of the pillared portico and the liveried servants who had been awaiting his arrival ran down to the phaeton.

The Butler, whom the Marquis had known as a child and who was now grey-haired and not as agile as he had once been, stopped on the last step.

"Welcome, M'Lord!" he said. "It is a great surprise

that you should visit us after so long, and I only hope we will make Your Lordship comfortable."

"I am sure you will, Newman," the Marquis said, "but I have with me an unexpected guest."

"A guest, M'Lord?" the Butler exclaimed in surprise, then following the direction of the Marquis's eyes he saw what lay on the floor of the phaeton.

"What has happened, M'Lord?"

"The villagers in Steeple were determined she was a witch!" the Marquis replied. "I saved her from having to endure the swimming test."

He spoke lightly but the Butler's face was serious as he said:

"Does Your Lordship suppose she's alive?"

The witch certainly looked dead as the scratches stood out vividly crimson on her pale face.

"She may not be!" the Marquis replied. "Let us take her inside and decide if it is worthwhile sending for a doctor."

The Butler snapped his fingers and two footmen went to the side of the phaeton.

They looked down at the witch, then instinctively they both took a step backwards.

"Pick her up!" the Marquis ordered.

Neither of the two young men made any attempt to obey him.

There was a faint smile on the Marquis's face as he asked:

"Are you afraid?"

"Aye, M'Lord!" one of the footmen replied with a broad Essex accent. "Oi dares not touch a witch, an' that's a fact!"

"And you?" the Marquis asked turning to the other.

"Me mother were cursed by a witch, M'Lord. Her were never th' same after it happened."

"Well, she can hardly stay here!" the Marquis said.

There was an amused expression on his face as he bent down and picked up the witch himself.

He thought as he did so that he had no desire to soil himself with the dirt that had stuck to her cloak, but unless he wished the whole household to be in a state of alarm he was aware he had to set an example.

Holding the girl in his arms he walked up the steps into the Hall, knowing that all the footmen were watching him wide-eyed.

"Well, Newman, where are we going to put her?" the Marquis asked.

The old Butler seemed to be confused.

"There's plenty of room in the servants' quarters, M'Lord," he answered a little hesitatingly, "but . ."

The Marquis well knew that he was thinking that to have the witch sleeping amongst them would send the servants into a panic.

Too late he thought he had been somewhat precipitous in bringing the witch to the Castle.

It would have been more prudent not to interfere and allow the villagers to deal with her as they thought best.

Then he told himself that such ignorant superstitions were ridiculous! They were living in civilised times.

How could they return to the bigotry and stupidity of those who believed in Satan and all his cohorts and were desperately afraid of sorcery?

Suddenly the Marquis had an idea.

"Is Nurse still here?" he enquired.

"Yes, of course, M'Lord. And in the Nursery, as she has always been."

"Then that, Newman, is the answer to the problem," the Marquis said and started to climb the wide staircase to the first floor.

It was fortunate that the witch was so light, because there were still two more floors for the Marquis to negotiate before finally he reached the third.

'Nothing has changed,' he thought.

There were the same rather low ceilings, the same pictures hanging on the walls, and when Newman hurried to open the door of the Nursery it was just as it had been when he had been a child.

The guard in front of the fire, the table with its thick, tasselled fringe in the centre of the room, the rocking-horse without a tail in the window, the fort which had been his delight until he was really too old to play with it, all were standing where they had always stood.

Sitting in a low chair, crocheting, was his old Nurse.

She had grown a little greyer and more lined than the Marquis remembered, but otherwise as she started to her feet in astonishment when she saw who stood there, she seemed as unchanged as the Nursery itself.

"Master Oswin!" she exclaimed. "I – I mean – Your Lordship!"

"You were expecting me, Nanny?" the Marquis asked.

"I was and I wasn't!" Nurse replied in a tone he knew only too well. "I doubted if you would have time for me!"

"I will always have time for you, Nanny," the Marquis replied, "and I have brought you someone who needs your help."

Nurse moved towards him to stare with astonishment at the woman he carried in his arms.

"Who is she? What has happened to her, M'Lord?"

"I have been told she is a witch!" the Marquis answered. "But she is not yet in a fit state to refute the allegation!"

"A witch?" Nurse exclaimed. "Stuff an' nonsense! Who's been filling your head with that sort of foolish talk?"

It was so like the remarks he had listened to as a child that the Marquis laughed.

"That is exactly what I thought you would say, Nanny. But the point is Newman thinks they would be frightened to have her in the servants' quarters, so I can only suggest that you look after her up here."

"I'll do that, M'Lord," Nurse said. "But I'll not have you putting her on one of my clean beds in that state, and that's a fact! Hold her a minute while I find something you can lay her on."

The old woman bustled into the Night-Nursery and the Marquis followed to watch her while she found an old sheet which she spread out over the bed.

"Now put her down, M'Lord," Nurse suggested. "She'll do no harm."

The Marquis did as he was told.

As he took his arms from around the girl he realised she had not stirred, and he thought, as he had done when he had seen her lying on the bottom of the phaeton, that she was very likely dead.

As if Nurse was thinking the same thing she picked up one thin wrist and put her fingers to it.

'Perhaps,' the Marquis thought, 'it was a good thing the witch was unconscious when the peasants found her!'

Some of the scratches on her arms were very deep and the nails that had made them had removed large pieces of skin.

He looked again at the mark on top of her head.

It had obviously been a heavy blow, a blow he was sure that had been meant to kill.

Had the old man been speaking the truth when he said that it had not been made by any of the villagers?

The Marquis was inclined to believe him.

It was not the habit of the peasants to kill witches by bludgeoning them.

They wanted the fun of testing them by swimming, of searching for the extra teat that was concealed on their bodies, by which they were supposed to feed their familiar.

And there had also been the amusement of sticking a needle into a witch to see if she would bleed.

The theory was that the Devil sealed his compact with a witch by giving her a mark on her body which was a token of his power.

If the mark was pricked and did not bleed, as warts rarely do, this was indisputable proof that she was a witch.

When the Marquis was in Scotland he had been shown one of the needles which had been used by the Witch Prickers for this test.

It was very sharp and had a handle. He was told that in some cases the needle used was retractable to make those who watched believe the woman was guilty because she did not bleed, while in fact the needle had not pierced her body at all!

One false Witch-Pricker was caught in Scotland and on the gallows confessed that he had caused the death of 220 women for the price of twenty shillings apiece.

The tortures of the 16th and 17th centuries were terrible and barbaric. Thumb screws, the rack, eye gougers, branding-irons and an apparatus known as

'The Question' which could dislocate every bone in the body, were all used.

Yet it seemed to the Marquis that the people who believed in witches were still as ignorant and cruel as they had been then.

There had been an atmosphere of hate and fear about the peasants of Steeple that was unmistakable.

He knew that even if the witch had sunk in the swimming test they would have seen to it that she was not alive when finally they had finished with her.

"Paganism dies hard!" he told himself.

"She's alive, M'Lord!" Nurse said putting the witch's hand down gently. "But only just!"

"Well, do your best for her, Nanny."

"I will, M'Lord! And don't you go a-listening to that heathen nonsense. They're ignorant creatures in this part of the world and always have been!"

"I remember your saying very much the same thing when I was a boy," the Marquis smiled.

"People don't change," Nurse answered. "They only get older!"

"That is true enough," the Marquis agreed, and he was smiling as he went downstairs.

3

"Tell me about the local trouble and unrest," the Marquis said to his agent.

Roger Clarke had recently taken over from his father who had been Agent at Ridge Castle for over thirty years.

He was a young man – not more than twenty-seven – but he was dedicated to his work and the Marquis knew that Mr. Graham thought highly of him.

"There has been trouble, My Lord, ever since Sir Harold died."

"Why?" the Marquis enquired.

He sat back in the high velvet arm-chair behind a huge flat-topped desk at which he remembered seeing his father sit on the few occasions he visited Ridge Castle.

But the Marquis knew it was his grandfather who had set the precedent that the Library, which was an extremely impressive room, should be the place where employees, tenants, farmers or anyone who sought his jurisdiction should be interviewed.

Nobody could have failed to note how distinguished the Marquis looked with a background of books and pictures set under the exquisitely painted ceiling.

It was a masterpiece executed by Italians who had been brought from Italy especially to work under one of the great artists chosen by Adam.

The long windows, framed with crimson velvet curtains, looked out onto the smooth lawns and the riot of flowers and almond bloom had been designed to achieve the maximum effect when viewed from the windows of the Castle.

Roger Clarke was young enough to appreciate and envy the Marquis's outstanding elegance in his grey whipcord riding-coat, his close fitting breeches and the manner in which his white stock was tied in a new style which must have been a headache to his valet.

As if the Marquis was conscious of the admiration in his Agent's eyes, he said:

"I must commend you, Clarke, for your reports which Mr. Graham has shown me. They are admirably written, concise and to the point."

"Thank you, My Lord," Roger Clarke said, colouring at the unexpected praise.

"And now tell me what Sir Caspar is doing to cause so much trouble."

"He has reduced wages for one thing, My Lord, and has stood off all the older men without an adequate pension, which means in most cases that they must starve or go on the Parish."

"Why should he have done that?" the Marquis asked sharply. "I always understood Sir Harold was a wealthy man."

"That is what we all thought, My Lord. But I cannot help suspecting that Sir Caspar needs the money either to redeem his debts or for further spending in London. He has no real interest in the country."

"How can you be sure of that?" the Marquis enquired.

"He has not come home, except at very irregular intervals, for years," Roger Clarke replied. "And it is local gossip that Sir Harold had continually begged him to return."

This only confirmed what the Marquis had thought about Caspar Trydell.

At the same time he knew how easy it was for the labourers to resent any change of employer, and he wondered if perhaps Sir Harold, in his old age and being ill, had grown lax.

"How are the estates run?" he enquired.

"They are in good heart, My Lord. The last manager was a conscientious fellow and I know for a fact that Sir Harold was very satisfied with him. Sir Caspar however sacked him on the ground that the yield from the fields was not high enough."

"Was that justified?"

"No, My Lord! We had a bad harvest last year and Your Lordship's returns were not up to their usual standard. Gales and torrential storms in the spring played havoc with the crops, as it did with the breeding of wild birds."

"I saw a good covey of partridges while I was coming here," the Marquis said.

"If this weather continues it will be the best nesting-season we have ever had," Mr. Roger Clarke said with a note of enthusiasm in his voice which the Marquis did not miss.

"You enjoy shooting?"

"Very much, My Lord. I have always been hoping that Your Lordship would honour us one September."

"I will think about it this year," the Marquis said.

As he spoke he remembered how he had enjoyed shooting with John Trydell.

It had been an inexpressible kindness on the elder boy's part to teach a lonely child, incarcerated in the great Castle with only a prosy Tutor to keep him company, how to shoot.

The Marquis had been ten at the time and it was John Trydell who had found him a small gun, explained carefully and patiently how he must carry it to be safe, how he must always unload before climbing over a hedge or fence, or crossing a stream.

The Marquis could still remember his excitement when he shot his first rabbit.

Afterwards there had been his first partridge, his first snipe, and most thrilling of all his first duck very early on a morning when dawn brought a flight in from the sea.

Nothing he had ever achieved in later life had quite equalled the elation of that moment when having fired his gun he waited breathlessly to see if the bird fell.

"I will certainly consider coming here either in September or October,' he said aloud.

"We shall look forward to it with great pleasure, My Lord," Roger Clarke replied and his tone was undoubtedly sincere.

"This afternoon I will ride out to the boundaries of the estate," the Marquis said. "I would like to visit the farm at Weatherwick. We have a good tenant there?"

"An excellent man, My Lord!"

"And we might be able to do Danely Farm at the same time."

"We, My Lord?"

"Naturally I shall expect you to accompany me," the Marquis answered, "and you can explain as we go exactly what you propose doing with the land we farm ourselves."

"I should be honoured, My Lord."

The Marquis rose to show that the interview was at an end but Roger Clarke hesitated.

"What is it?" the Marquis enquired.

"I hope you will not think it impertinent, My Lord, but everyone is talking of how you rescued the witch from being ducked at Steeple."

"I imagined it would give them something to chatter about," the Marquis said with a faint smile.

"I was wondering if Your Lordship had any idea of the identity of the woman in question?"

"None at all!" the Marquis answered. "She has not yet regained consciousness. Someone, Clarke, and I intend to find out who it was, hit her a blow on the head which would have killed a normal woman."

"Do you think one of the villagers who had found her, did it, My Lord?"

"I doubt it," the Marquis replied. "As they were dragging her to the duck pond it would have spoilt their amusement if she had been already dead! I thought that, although they were obviously activated by hatred and fear, they were not the sort to commit murder!"

"No, indeed, My Lord. They are simple folk, and as Your Lordship knows, extremely superstitious, but that is true of everyone in Essex."

Roger Clarke grinned.

"No one has forgotten the first witch trial at Chelmsford when Elizabeth Francis pleaded guilty."

"To what? — I have forgotten the details," the Marquis said.

"To bewitching a child, My Lord, so that he became decrepit. Elizabeth Francis had learnt her witchcraft from her grandmother. She had renounced God and her familiar was a white cat called Satan."

The Marquis looked sceptical and Roger Clarke went on:

"The cat, speaking in a hollow voice, promised her both riches and a husband. He demonstrated his prowess by killing a man who had refused to respond to her advances."

"And the Court believed this?" the Marquis enquired.

"She admitted that with the assistance of the cat she killed a child and secured herself a husband. She then murdered her own baby."

"Good Lord!" the Marquis exclaimed.

"Elizabeth passed on her cat in exchange for a cake, to a Mother Waterhouse, who sent Satan to drown a neighbour's cow, kill his geese, spoil butter, and commit murder."

"If I remember correctly, Mother Waterhouse was the first woman in England to be hanged for witchcraft," the Marquis remarked.

"That's right, My Lord, to be followed by hundreds more."

"It all happened a long time ago."

"To the peasants it happened yesterday! They still whisper about Elizabeth Bennett who confessed to having two belligerent imps who held her prisoner for hours and tried to push her into the oven!"

The Marquis laughed.

"Can they really believe such nonsense?"

"They do indeed, My Lord. Any cow that sickens is thought to be a victim of the evil eye, and sow-fever is ascribed to the direct action of the Devil! I am sure they still make figurines of clay in the likeness of an enemy and stick pins in them to create pain and even death."

"Surely we have taught people a little more sense in the last two hundred years?"

"I doubt it, My Lord," Roger Clarke replied, "and certainly not as far as Essex is concerned. Your Lordship will recall that we here are not far from the Witch Country."

"The Witch Country?" the Marquis repeated in a puzzled tone.

"The part of South-East Essex divided from us only by the River Crouch is known as the Witch Country, My Lord."

"I was not aware of that," the Marquis said.

"The whole population, irrespective of social position, is obsessed by fears of wizards and witches," Roger Clarke explained. "Ghosts haunt the fields and the Devil has been known to chase a parson from the pulpit."

The Marquis raised his eye-brows.

"Of course there are white witches and wizards who cure warts, find lost and stolen property, and remove evil spells."

"I am glad to hear it," the Marquis remarked dryly.

"My father was once given a 'holey' stone as a charm to ward off witches," Roger Clarke went on. "Perhaps I should lend it to Your Lordship."

For a second the Marquis stiffened as if he thought the suggestion an impertinence.

Then he laughed.

"I will chance it!" he said. "What are they saying locally will happen to me because I saved a so-called witch from the duck pond?"

"They are waiting to see if Your Lordship dies, or if the Castle falls down."

The Marquis laughed again.

"The witch is a young girl not more than eighteen," he said, "and of gentle birth. Quite frankly, Clarke, the position is this: she has been diabolically treated by someone who wished her dead and I am determined to find out who it is."

Roger Clarke looked startled.

"Do you think it was a deliberate attempt at murder, My Lord?"

"I am sure of it!" the Marquis replied. "Nurse assures me that if the girl had not been using a number of strongly-made hairpins to keep her hair in order, she would undoubtedly have died from the blow on her head."

The Marquis paused to add:

"As it was, two hairpins were driven deep into the skin, but they saved her life."

"I cannot understand it, My Lord," Roger Clarke said. "I know this part of the world, and I can think of no young girl who answers to that description. And certainly not one of gentle birth."

"Are you sure of that?"

"Quite sure. As Your Lordship can imagine, since I have lived here all my life, a strange face causes quite a sensation and is something one does not forget easily!"

He smiled before he went on:

"As you will understand, My Lord, the witch is now thought to be an evil spirit of surpassing beauty who has bewitched Your Lordship!"

The Marquis was following his own train of thought, and after a moment he said:

"Only a man or a woman of great strength could have inflicted such a deep wound on the girl's head. Also to screw the neck off a young cock would have been beyond the strength of the girl upstairs!"

"But why should any man have wanted to murder a young girl," Roger Clarke asked, "then lay her on the

Druid stones? If he were a local, he would have known it would immediately arouse the peasants' fear of witch-craft."

"I have already thought it was a deliberate action, myself," the Marquis remarked.

He walked across the Library to stand at the window looking out onto the sunny garden.

After a moment he said:

"I want you to make enquiries, Clarke, as to whether anyone the night before this girl was found, saw anything strange in the village of Steeple or in the country round about."

The Marquis paused before he went on:

"Do you think for instance there might have been smugglers landing at Lawling Creek that night and the girl surprised them?"

"That is a possibility, My Lord, except that Law-ling Creek is quite a step from the Druid stones. It seems unlikely that any smuggler would take the trouble to carry her there."

"I agree, unless they wished to ensure that the crime was not connected with them."

The Marquis thought for a moment. Then he said:

"If I had not happened to pass Steeple at the exact moment when the peasants were dragging the unfortunate girl to the pond, she would have been drowned and no-one would ever have heard any more about her."

"That is true, My Lord," Roger Clarke agreed. "Then as likely as not she would have been buried at the cross-roads with her head facing north. Unless of course they decided to throw her into the sea at Steeple Creek, which has happened before now."

"It has?" the Marquis questioned with interest.

"It may only be gossip, My Lord, but there have been many stories of how when men fought over local feuds the loser has landed upon the sands with no evidence to prove he died in any other way except by drowning."

"That makes the river extremely convenient for the people who live here!" the Marquis said dryly.

"Exactly, My Lord!"

"Well, make what enquiries you can, Clarke," the Marquis ordered. "I shall expect you at the front door at one o'clock with the horses. Give the order to the stables, I will ride the stallion."

"I will tell them, My Lord."

Roger Clarke bowed and left the Library.

The Marquis still stood at the wondow.

There was a frown between his eyes as he apparently contemplated the pink almond blossom petals drifting softly onto the grass.

Then, as if he made up his mind, he walked resolutely from the Library and up the stairs to the Nursery.

It was now the second day since he had rescued the witch from the villagers, and he was well aware that the fact that she was staying in the Castle had caused something like consternation amongst his staff.

The Housekeeper had reported to him two cases of hysteria amongst the younger maids and he could see the footmen who were all local lads eyeing him apprehensively when they were on duty in the Hall or serving in the Dining-Room.

It was almost as if they expected him to grow horns or cloven hoofs, the Marquis thought with a smile, simply because he had been in contact with a witch!

As he entered the Nursery, Nurse, who had been preparing something on the table, looked up.

It seemed to the Marquis that she had grown younger since his return and he was sure it was because he had found her something to do.

'It must,' he thought with a sudden perception, 'be very frustrating to sit for years with idle hands in an empty Nursery.'

"I was hoping you would visit me, M'Lord," Nurse said. "I've something to show you."

"Your patient has recovered consciousness?"

"No, M'Lord, but she's breathing more naturally and passed a quiet night. I shouldn't be surprised if she wakes any time now."

"I still think you should have let me send for a physician."

"What would have been the use?" Nurse asked. "He's nothing but an old saw-bones whom I would not trust to set a broken finger, let alone treat an affliction of the mind!"

The scathing note in Nurse's voice made the Marquis smile.

He knew of old of her sentiments when it came to doctors, and he remembered when he was a boy, however ill he might be, she would never allow one in the Castle.

He looked down at the table and seeing a number of herbs he knew that Nurse was preparing one of her famous tisanes.

"You know, Nanny," he said jokingly, "it would never surprise me if you were ducked for being a witch! If you had not had the protection of the Castle walls. I am convinced it would have happened long ago!"

"More than likely!" Nurse agreed complacently. "As long as there are ignorant, half-witted people around, who believe that anyone who uses nature's

69

method of healing is in league with the Devil, anything might happen!"

"And what magic potion is this that the poor, wretched girl will have to swallow?" the Marquis teased.

"It is something that will do her good, Master Oswin," Nurse said tartly, "and that's all you need to know!"

The Marquis smiled.

"But that wasn't what I wanted to show you."

Nurse put down the knife with which she was chopping the herbs and went to the white chest-of-drawers which stood against the far end of the Nursery.

From the top of it she picked up a handkerchief and brought it to the Marquis for his inspection.

"I found this in the pocket of her gown. I've washed and pressed it. As Your Lordship sees, it tells us her Christian name."

The Marquis looked at the handkerchief with interest.

It was a very fine muslin and he could see that it had been neatly hemmed.

In one corner embroidered very skilfully with tiny stitches that might have been made by fairy fingers was a name.

"Idylla!" the Marquis said aloud. "That, unless I am mistaken, comes from the Greek word which suggests perfection. It would seem, Nanny, that our visitor thinks well of herself!"

"Or rather, her parents thought well of her, M'Lord!" Nurse corrected. "I don't suppose she chose her own name."

"No, of course not," the Marquis admitted.

He wondered if it was a clue to which Roger Clarke would have the answer.

There could not be many women in this part of the

70

country called Idylla, which was in fact a name he himself had never met before.

While he was looking at the handkerchief Nurse had opened the door of the Night-Nursery and gone inside.

Now the Marquis heard her call him. "My Lord!"

There was something urgent in her voice which made him walk quickly into the room.

The blind was half-lowered to keep out the brilliance of the sunshine. Nevertheless it was easy to see clearly the figure lying in the narrow bed, her head against a white pillow.

The girl's hair was dark and silky against the sheets which Nurse had pulled nearly up to her chin.

Framed by it, her face with its pointed chin looked somehow ethereal and insubstantial despite the scratches that were still visible on her cheeks.

The Marquis had seen her yesterday after she had been washed and he had thought then that she looked so fragile that he would not be surprised if she died during the night.

Now as he looked down, half-expecting that she was in fact dead, he realised that Nurse had called him for a very different reason.

Idylla, if that was her name, had her eyes open.

The Marquis looked at her. He had expected, simply because she had been called a witch, that her eyes would be green; instead they were surprisingly a vivid blue.

It was such an unusual combination with dark hair and dark eye-lashes that they made her seem quite unlike anyone he had ever seen before.

"You are awake!" Nurse said gently. "There is no need to be frightened. I will give you something to drink."

She turned to the table at the side of the bed as she spoke and the Marquis saw she had prepared one of the healing potions which she invariably gave to anyone who was ill.

He could recall the sweet taste of them since Nurse had always disguised the many herbs she used with the sweetness of honey. The Marquis remembered being only too willing to drink down as many glasses as she wished to give him.

Idylla's eyes seemed not to have moved since the Marquis had first looked at her, and he had the impression that she was not seeing clearly, only staring at the light.

Then as Nurse put her arm behind her and lifted her a little so as to hold the cup to her lips, she made a little sound as if of pain.

She drank from the cup at first tentatively, then took several sips before Nurse laid her back against the pillows.

"That's better!" she said soothingly. "Now go to sleep."

As if she was willing to obey the note of command in Nurse's voice, Idylla closed her eyes.

Once again the Marquis noted how long and dark her eye-lashes were against the transparency of her cheeks. Then when it was obvious that she had fallen asleep he turned and walked quietly from the Night-Nursery.

Nurse followed him.

"You see, M'Lord? There was no need for any blundering physician. She'll be all right in a day or two."

"As I have said before," the Marquis replied, "you are an old witch, Nanny. I was quite right to leave her in your capable hands."

"You can be sure of that," Nurse replied, "and I'll

tell you one thing, M'Lord. If we know nothing else about Miss Idylla, she's a lady born and bred."

"How can you be sure of that?" the Marquis asked.

"It's not only her looks, M'Lord, her long fingers and her well-arched insteps, which are signs of the type of stock she's come from. It's her clothes!"

"Her clothes?" the Marquis questioned.

"Everything she was wearing under her gown, M'Lord, was handmade by someone who understands how to sew properly. Something the girls to-day are seldom taught! Beautifully made her things are, and edged with lace. Not very expensive, mind you! But they're the choice only a lady would make. I assure you, M'Lord, I know what I'm talking about!"

"I can well believe that, Nanny."

"And mark my words, M'Lord, when you find out who Miss Idylla is, she may prove to be a Princess in disguise!"

Now the Marquis threw back his head and laughed.

"You are not only a witch, Nanny, you are also a romantic!"

"And why not?" the Nurse asked truculently. "Not that it's any use my being romantic as far as you're concerned, M'Lord. Every time there's been a letter from London I've hoped and prayed to hear news of an engagement."

"Good Heavens!" the Marquis exclaimed. "Why have you been so intent upon marrying me off?"

"Because it's only natural that you should settle down and rear a family. You're thirty, Master Oswin. Time most gentlemen are Christening their third or fourth! But you without one to your name, and me waiting with an empty cradle!"

The Marquis laughed again.

"Even to please you, Nanny, and to fill your empty cradle I refuse to shackle myself to some tiresome young woman who will undoubtedly prove to be a dead bore as soon as the honeymoon is over."

There was a cynical note in the Marquis's voice which made his old Nurse look at him sharply.

"Now come along, Master Oswin!" she said. "You're not telling me you've not a wide choice."

"Who has been talking?" the Marquis enquired.

"We're not so benighted at the Castle that we don't hear what's going on in London," Nurse snapped. "And that's plenty, if I'm not mistaken! You're not your father's son for nothing!"

The Marquis stiffened.

He always disliked references to his father's amatory adventures which had been the talk of the previous generation, just as his occupied the minds of the present one.

Then he knew that Nurse, who had loved him ever since he was a baby, was perhaps the only woman in the world who desired his happiness utterly unselfishly.

If any other woman who cared for him prayed for his happiness. it was only because it would include herself.

Apart from the obvious desire of Nanny to hold his son in her arms, she loved him, as the Marquis knew, with a devotion that was entirely maternal.

He could not remember his mother who had died when he was three years old, and it was Nanny who had given him the only affection he knew during the years while his father ignored him whenever possible.

She had cosseted and scolded him, spoiled and punished him. She had taught him his first lessons, and even when he had thought himself too old to have a Nurse she had always been there in the background.

Someone who waited as eagerly for him to return from school as he longed to escape from it!

He realised, as he was thinking, that Nurse had been looking at him with eyes which missed little.

"You have grown hard and cynical, Master Oswin," she said. "What you want in your life is love!"

"There is too much of that," the Marquis replied quickly.

"Not of the right sort, I'll be bound!"

And because invariably Nanny had the last word, he could not help smiling.

"You are right – you are always right!" he said. "They have not been the right sort, Nanny, and that is why I have come home to you."

"That's sensible," Nurse said with satisfaction. "What you want is plenty to occupy your mind and something to do, M'Lord, and I don't mean all those high jinks which occupy you in London! Too much drinking and too many late hours are very bad for you, as you well know!"

"As I well know!" the Marquis repeated.

"You'll find plenty here to keep you busy, if you look for it," the Nurse said. "And when you have time, find out about Miss Idylla. If there's one think I dislike it's a mystery!"

"That is exactly what I intend to do," the Marquis answered and went downstairs.

He had not missed the fact that Nurse had perfected her patient's name with the respectful 'Miss'.

He was well aware that this was something he should intimate to the rest of the household, and when he reached the Hall he said to the Butler:

"I know you will be glad to hear, Newman, that Nurse has discovered the Christian name of our visitor."

"Indeed, M'Lord?"

"It is Idylla, and you may inform the household that in future the young lady upstairs will be referred to by everyone as Miss Idylla."

"Very good, M'Lord."

The Butler hesitated a moment, then he said:

"Two of the lads from the village, M'Lord, have asked permission to terminate their employment, and Mrs. Darwin tells me one of the under-housemaids also wishes to leave."

"Let them go and fill their places with those who are not so bigoted and uncivilised."

The Marquis raised his voice a little as he went on, so that the footmen on duty in the Hall could hear what he said.

"Let me make this quite clear, Newman. If a servant does not show any guest in my house, whoever he or she may be, the utmost respect whether in their presence or not, then I shall expect the senior staff to dismiss them immediately! Is that understood?"

"I'll convey your instructions, M'Lord, both to Mrs. Darwin and to Mrs. Headley in the kitchen."

"Tell Mrs. Headley that the food I have enjoyed so far has been excellent!" the Marquis said. "I have never eaten better salmon than the one that was served last night."

"Thank you, M'Lord! I'm sure Mrs. Headley will be very gratified. She's been extremely nervous, as Your Lordship will understand, that the food at the Castle might not measure up to the standard Your Lordship enjoys in Berkeley Square!"

"The two are incomparable," the Marquis said. "Kindly reassure Mrs. Headley that I am not only extremely pleased with the meals she has served so far, but

I am also finding them a very pleasant change!"

"Thank you, M'Lord! Thank you very much!" the Butler beamed.

.   .   .   .   .

It was late in the evening before the Marquis, having ridden many miles with Roger Clarke, returned to the Castle tired, but having, as he admitted to himself, thoroughly enjoyed the afternoon.

It was not only the feeling of well-being he had from riding his magnificent stallion over the flat unspoilt country with the sea-breeze in his face and the joy of being untrammelled and unconstrained which he had not experienced for many years.

It was also the manner in which he had been welcomed by the farmers and their wives, from whom he had learnt that they appreciated their tenancies and were well content to farm on the Ridge Estate.

Several of the farmers had known the Marquis's father. Although the previous Marquis had many faults, he had been a good landlord and took a pride in seeing that on his Estates his tenants were happy and not at odds with the owner.

"You know, M'Lord," Roger Clarke said as they rode home, "if the whole of England followed the example of the Ridge Estates, I cannot help feeling we would be free from much of the trouble which incites people to violence and ends in protestors breaking windows and booing Members of Parliament in Whitehall."

"I am afraid it is the Prince of Wales who gets booed most frequently," the Marquis remarked.

"And with reason!" Roger Clarke remarked adding

quickly: "I apologise, M'Lord. I spoke without thinking!"

"You spoke what you believe to be the truth," the Marquis said. "At the same time, the Prince is really more sinned against than sinning. Although you may find it hard to believe, he has little chance at the moment to do anything but waste his life seeking pleasure when, if he had his way, he would be engaged in much more serious pursuits."

The Marquis was thinking as he spoke of how the Prince two years earlier had entertained high hopes of being appointed Lord Lieutenant of Ireland.

It was an idea suggested to him by the Irish Whigs but the King had discounted it out of hand and the Prince had said despairingly:

"My father complains about my extravagance, he moans incessantly about my way of life, but if I ever have an idea of doing anything else, it is slapped down as if I were a naughty schoolboy!"

There was no gainsaying this and the Marquis had in fact been very sympathetic.

Seeing the extravagance of Carlton House parties, hearing only the gossip about the Prince's innumerable love-affairs, it was no wonder that the country as a whole thought of him as a drunken dilettante and had no idea he had many more serious qualities.

Back at the Castle the Marquis bathed, changed for dinner and went down to dine alone in the large Dining-Room painted exquisitely with murals of allegorical scenes. He was alone but he did not feel lonely.

What he did feel was extremely hungry.

He knew that such strenuous exercise was something which he had needed for a long time, but which he could never find by galloping around the parks of

London, or driving his phaeton to a Mill at Wimbledon or the races at Newmarket.

There were many more of his farms yet for him to see, he told himself with satisfaction, and did full justice to the many delicious dishes that Mrs. Headley had prepared for him.

When he finished he decided he would go to the Library to see if there were any books there on witchcraft.

He was certain there would be some reference to witches in the *History of Essex*, and he had a feeling that somewhere he had read about the famous magician, Dr. Dee, who had been called Queen Elizabeth's Merlin.

Unless his memory was at fault Dr. Dee had been in trouble in Mary's reign for casting a horoscope of the Queen at the request of someone at Court.

He had been acquitted and had become a great favourite of Elizabeth when she came to the throne.

'Perhaps the history of Dr. Dee will throw some light on what is puzzling me,' the Marquis thought.

He was sure that the more he learnt about witchcraft the more likely he was to discover the reason Idylla had been left on the Druid stones with a sacrificial cock bleeding on her gown.

As he rose to leave the Dining-Room the Butler said to him:

"Excuse me, M'Lord, but Nurse asked me to inform Your Lordship that Miss Idylla is conscious."

This was interesting, the Marquis thought, and would undoubtedly tell him far more about his involuntary guest than any book could do.

He hurried up the stairs and reached the Nursery on the third floor without losing breath.

Nurse heard him open the Day-Nursery door and came from the bed-room.

"She's properly awake, M'Lord!" she said triumphantly. "I've not questioned her. I thought Your Lordship might wish to do that."

"Of course," the Marquis answered.

He walked into the Night-Nursery, looking very large and tall in the low-ceilinged room.

Although it was not yet dark outside the candles had been lit beside Idylla's bed and the light from them illumined her small face and seemed to linger in her blue eyes.

Again the Marquis thought how strange she looked.

Her eyes were not even the pale blue one might have expected, but the deep, vivid blue of gentians or the Southern sea on a sunny day; fringed with dark lashes, they had a beauty that was indescribable.

She was not in the least like a witch, the Marquis decided, but rather like a nymph who had risen from the depths of a still lake, or perhaps a white-crested wave to bewilder and beguile the human beings who beheld her.

Then he told himself he was being absurdly poetic and walked purposefully towards the bed to sit down on the wicker chair which Nanny had placed in position for him.

Idylla seemed to be looking at him gravely and perhaps speculatively; but she did not appear frightened and after a moment he said:

"I am afraid you have been through a very unpleasant experience, but you are quite safe here in my house."

"Where..am..I?"

Her voice was very low and hesitant as if she found it hard to speak, but it was musical and educated.

Her thin, sensitive hands lay in front of her on the sheets, and the Marquis thought as he glanced at them and heard her voice that he had been quite right in thinking she was well-born, and a gentle-woman.

"You are at Ridge Castle," he replied to her question.

"R . Ridge . . Castle?" She repeated the words as if she was trying to remember if they meant anything to her.

"You have heard of it?" the Marquis asked softly.

"I . . do not . . think so."

"Then suppose we start at the beginning?" the Marquis suggested. "We know your name is Idylla. It was embroidered on the handkerchief Nurse found in the pocket of your gown. And very beautifully embroidered too!"

"May I . . see it?"

As if she had already anticipated the question, Nanny had the handkerchief handy and gave it to Idylla.

She looked at it, turning the embroidered name towards the light.

"You say this is . . mine?" she asked after a moment.

"You do not recognise it?" the Marquis asked.

"I do . . not . . think so."

"But your name is Idylla?"

She looked at him and for the first time he saw an expression of fear in her eyes.

"I do not . . know," she answered. "I cannot . . remember who I am or . . anything about . . myself."

The Marquis looked at her in astonishment.

"How do you know that?"

"I have been . . thinking this afternoon when I was . . awake," she answered. "The room was . . strange and my head hurt, so I thought I must have had an . . accident. But I cannot remember it."

"You cannot remember anything hitting you on the head?" the Marquis asked.

"No," she replied.

"Then can you remember your home — where you live?"

"It is very . . strange," she said slowly. "When I try to . . think about myself or . . where I have come from everything is . . dark. It is just like a . . black curtain between . . to-day and . . yesterday."

Her voice was so troubled that the Marquis smiled at her reassuringly.

"This is what we might have expected after a blow such as you received," he said. "You must have fallen and perhaps struck something inadvertently. Whatever it was, it rendered you unconscious and you have lost your memory."

"Will it . . come back?"

"But of course!" he replied. "It is quite a usual symptom of concussion. It happened to me once when I had a fall out hunting. For twenty-four hours I could not remember what had happened, and I was told later I was delirious."

"I . . I have not been . . delirious?" Idylla said. "At least I do not . . think so."

She glanced at Nurse as she spoke.

"No, dear, you've been as quiet as a little mouse ever since you came here," Nurse said.

"You . . tell me . . this is . . Ridge Castle," Idylla said rather like a child repeating her first lesson at school.

"That is correct," the Marquis replied.

"Who . . are . . you?"

"I am the Marquis of Aldridge."

He almost expected some flicker of recognition in her eyes such as he had seen so often in other women's.

Instead Idylla regarded him gravely, and there was not even that glint of admiration and enticement to which he was so used, and which, now that it was not there, he missed.

"It is very .. kind of you to .. have me. I would not .. wish to be a .. nuisance."

"You are certainly not that," the Marquis answered. "But now I think you should go to sleep again. The more you rest, the quicker your memory will return."

"You are .. certain that it will?"

"Of course I am certain," the Marquis answered. "Then you will be able to tell me if you wish me to notify anyone of your whereabouts, perhaps your mother or father. They will be very worried that you have disappeared."

"How can .. I have done .. that?"

"I have no idea," the Marquis replied, "but I hope you will soon be able to tell me exactly what happened to you. So get well quickly. I shall be as interested as you are to have an explanation of how you injured your head."

He rose from the chair and smiled down at her as if she were a child.

"Good-night, Idylla. Just go to sleep and your memory will come back. That I promise you. Good-night, Nanny."

He went downstairs with a smile on his lips, well assured that his curiosity about his strange guest would soon be assuaged.

At least he was certain of one thing: Idylla, whoever she might be, was not a witch but in fact a very bewitching and attractive young woman!

4

The Marquis was permitting his Valet to help him into his riding-coat when there was a knock on the door.

On the dressing-table lay several crumpled cravats which had not been tied to his liking.

The one he wore was perfect, exactly the width, height and twist ordained by Beau Brummell who had invented that particular style.

As the Marquis pulled his coat into place he knew that it was a trifle looser than it had been when he first wore it. As if he realised what his Master was thinking, the Valet said:

"You've lost weight, M'Lord. Your Lordship's taking more exercise than you do in London."

"That is true, Harris," the Marquis agreed, "and incidentally drinking less."

"It becomes you, M'Lord."

As the Marquis did not reply the Valet went on:

"Quite a number of Your Lordship's clothes will have to be altered when we return to London if they are to fit to 'perfection' as Mr. Weston requires."

Weston was the tailor patronised by the Prince of Wales, and the majority of the Rakes and Dandies who followed the Royal lead.

The Marquis suddenly remembered there had been a knock at the door.

"Come in!" he said and saw it was Nurse who wished to enter.

"May I speak to Your Lordship?" she asked.

"Of course, Nanny," he replied as his Valet tactfully withdrew. "How is our patient this morning?"

"She's better in health, M'Lord, but there's still no sign of her memory returning. It worries her, although I keep telling her it's quite natural."

"Of course it is!" the Marquis said. "After a blow like that she must expect to suffer from concussion for quite a time, and I am sure if it were not for your care of her she would be far worse."

"I thought that myself, M'Lord," Nurse answered, "but that's not the reason I came to see you."

"What is it?" the Marquis enquired.

As he stood waiting for her to speak, she thought it would be difficult to imagine a finer figure of a man.

She had always been proud of her 'baby' as she called the Marquis to herself.

He had been an unusually handsome and singularly attractive child, but even she had not imagined that he would grow up into quite such a striking figure as he was now.

"Well, Nanny?" the Marquis prompted impatiently.

"I was thinking, M'Lord, that what Miss Idylla needs is fresh air, and I was wondering if Your Lordship would give permission for her to use Her Ladyship's bedroom which has a balcony."

The Marquis knew that Nurse was speaking of his grandmother, for as far as he knew his mother had never visited Ridge Castle.

When William Adam, father of Robert and James, had practically completed the Castle, his grandfather and grandmother had moved in to superintend the decoration of the State Rooms by the Italian artists and to choose the furniture and pictures.

In all his buildings, which were numerous, the third Marquis liked to complete in every detail whatever house engaged his fancy at the moment.

He had made improvement to Aldridge Park in Oxfordshire, but there had not been as much building to do there as on the other estates which had been added to the family possessions.

At the time everyone had thought it grossly extravagant to spend so much money on so many different buildings.

But there was no doubt that everything the third Marquis had bought in the way of furniture and pictures had grown more valuable as time passed and would doubtless continue to do so.

His wife had not been a strong woman and in middle age had developed arthritis of the hip which prevented her from walking easily and finally kept her confined to a wheel-chair.

After the Castle was finished her husband had added a large balcony to one of the State bed-rooms on the first floor. This enabled her to sit in the sunshine overlooking the garden without always having to be carried downstairs.

Since the present Marquis had inherited the title the room had never been used, and he thought now it was an excellent idea for Idylla to sleep there and be able to sit outside without any exertion on her part.

"Of course you are right, Nanny," he said aloud. "I should have thought of it myself. Tell Mrs. Darwin to have the room prepared, and Miss Idylla can be taken there as soon as it is ready."

"Thank you, M'Lord," the Nurse said.

Then with a smile she added:

"There is however one problem Your Lordship has not thought about."

"What is that?" the Marquis asked.

He turned from the dressing-table to pick up a handkerchief, and now he was ready to descend the stairs to breakfast, aware that his horse would be waiting for him outside the Castle as soon as he was finished.

"It is unlikely that anyone in the household will consent to carry Miss Idylla downstairs," Nurse replied. "They are not as scared of her as they were but I doubt if there is a man amongst them who would touch a witch!"

The Marquis laughed.

"That leaves me to do what you require, Nanny. All right, when I come back from riding I will carry our guest to her new room. If I fall down or turn into a toad we shall know she really is a witch!"

"Thank you, M'Lord," Nanny said, "and just one more thing."

"Another?"

The Marquis had already walked towards the door and now he turned back.

"I don't suppose Your Lordship, being a man, has thought that Miss Idylla has nothing to wear when she is well enough to get up. Her gown was practically torn to pieces, and even if I tried I doubt if I could wash the blood from it."

Nurse paused before she said with her eyes twinkling:

"I've lent her my nightgowns, but I hardly think my clothes would look right on a lady young enough to be my grandchild."

"I thought I had an eye for detail and a capacity for organisation," the Marquis said, "but you put me to shame, Nanny."

"You'll see to it, M'Lord?"

"I will see to it," he said firmly. "Have you her measurements?"

Nurse drew a piece of paper from the pocket of her white apron.

"I thought perhaps if you sent a groom to Chelmsford," she said, "he would find a ready-made gown or two, besides the other things I've listed."

The Marquis took the piece of paper.

"You can leave it to me."

"You know what to ask for?" Nurse enquired.

There was a twinkle in the Marquis's eyes as he replied:

"You are assuming that I am unversed in the requirements of the fair sex, Nanny," he answered. "An assumption quite unrelated to fact!"

Before she could reply he ran downstairs carrying her list in his hands.

Instead of turning towards the Breakfast-Room where Newman and two footmen were waiting to serve him from a quite inordinate choice of well-prepared dishes, the Marquis went to the Library.

He sat down at his desk, read Nurse's memorandum carefully, then set a piece of writing-paper ready on the open blotter.

As he did so he was wondering what colours would best become Idylla.

As it happened he knew a great deal about feminine attire, not only because he had paid so many bills for so many different types of women.

When he was young one of his mistresses had been

88

an exceedingly attractive ballerina of Russian birth.

She had an unusual beauty and a grace which was outstanding as the Marquis had realised when he saw her dance.

But he found that owing to her strict training and the fact that until he had discovered her she had enjoyed little success in her private life, Talika dressed badly.

At a passing glance she appeared insignificant when she was not on the stage.

It had amused the Marquis to take her to the most expensive Couturiers and dress her in a manner which made her gowns a frame for her beauty.

They made so much difference to her appearance that while at first the Marquis's friends had been rather surprised at him favouring Talika, they then tried in every possible way to entice her away from him.

That would have been impossible until the Marquis tired of her, but by that time she was an assured success not only in the ballet, but also among the gentlemen of St. James's.

"How was it possible for you alone to perceive Talika's beauty and potential talents?" one nobleman who was noted for pursuing every new Venus enquired.

"A fine jewel needs to be well set," the Marquis had replied and he told himself that was true of all women.

He wrote now a note to a dressmaker who was not only patronised by the ladies of the *Beau Monde* but also had an original and creative mind which made her sought out by many theatrical producers.

In his letter the Marquis described Idylla's strange beauty, her dark hair and blue eyes and also the slenderness of her figure, giving the measurements that Nurse had taken.

He told Madame Valerie, as she was called, exactly what he required.

He made it clear that the groom was not to return empty-handed, although when she sent notification that the rest of the order was ready it would be fetched from London.

It was quite a long letter and the Marquis was satisfied when he had finished that Madame Valerie would carry out his wishes exactly.

He sealed it with a wafer and carried it into the Hall where he instructed a footman to send it to the stables immediately so that a groom could set out for London without delay.

Feeling satisfied with the trouble he had taken he went in to breakfast.

The Marquis had made no plans for the morning and after he had ridden for an hour and a half he returned to the Castle and climbed to the third floor.

Nurse looked surprised when he entered the Day-Nursery.

"You're back already, M'Lord? I was not expecting you so soon."

"I am having an early luncheon," the Marquis replied. "If Miss Idylla is not yet ready I can wait."

"Mrs. Darwin told me half an hour ago that Her Ladyship's room has been opened and the bed aired," Nurse replied. "As Your Lordship well knows, the rooms are always kept in order in case you should wish to use them."

"You are implying that it has been a disappointment to the staff that I have not been to the Castle for so long."

"It's a disappointment to me too," the Nurse said, "but you're here now and that's all that matters! Just wait a moment while I get Miss Idylla ready for Your Lordship."

She went into the Night-Nursery as she spoke and shut the door.

The Marquis looked at the china ornaments on the mantelpiece and the portrait of himself which stood above it.

It had been painted when he was twelve and showed him with his gun under his arm and a spaniel sitting at his feet.

It had been done more or less for amusement by an artist from London on holiday, and was well executed. The Marquis had bought it quite cheaply to give to his father for Christmas.

But when the time came he decided his father would not appreciate the effort he had had to make to stand still for so many hours, and was unlikely anyway to want a portrait of his son.

He had therefore presented it to Nanny who had been thrilled with the gift and hung it in the place of honour in the Nursery.

Now as he looked at it the Marquis remembered once again the thrill of learning to shoot.

When John Trydell could not go with him he would set off alone with his dog, a game-bag over his shoulders, delighted when he could return with two or three trophies as proof of his marksmanship.

The Marquis thought now of all the shooting he had done since then in other parts of the country, when a big bag had been the result at the end of the day.

Nothing had given him more satisfaction than the times he had shot here when the winter would have seemed long and cold and sometimes very dreary without shooting to keep him amused.

"We are ready, M'Lord," Nurse's voice said behind him and he walked across the Nursery into the bedroom.

Idylla was lying on top of the bed and the Marquis saw that Nurse had enveloped her in white blankets so that she looked like a cocoon.

He was quite certain that it was not only for the sake of warmth but was also an effort at modesty.

He looked down at her small face peeping from among the blankets and saw that Nurse had tied her hair neatly on either side of her face with ribbons which matched her eyes.

"Good morning, Idylla," the Marquis said in his deep voice.

"Good .. morning .. My Lord," she replied a little breathlessly.

He had a feeling she was embarrassed, and to set her at her ease he said:

"You must not be frightened that I shall drop you. We will go very carefully down the stairs, and I am sure Nanny is right and you will find the room to which I am taking you much more comfortable than this one."

As he spoke he put his arms around her and lifted her as if she were a child.

He remembered as he did so how light she had been when he carried her upstairs covered with mud and filth after he had rescued her from the villagers.

He saw now that the scratches on her face were fading. They were still visible, but they were no longer open sores and there was every likelihood that in a few days they would disappear.

The Marquis started slowly to descend the stairs which were not very wide.

He thought as he went it was only the second time he

had ever carried a woman in his arms not for some amorous purpose.

Idylla lay very still. She did not look up at him but watched the way ahead, and yet he had the feeling that she was shyly conscious of him as a man.

"She is very young," the Marquis told himself.

He wondered if in fact she had a *Beau* to make love to her and tell her how beautiful she was.

Unless, he thought, she had been brought up in a lonely part of the country where there were few young men, or incarcerated in a convent, it would be impossible for her beauty to go unnoticed.

He found the curiosity he had about her growing even more acute than it had in the last few days.

Who was she? Where did she come from? What was her name? And why, as he had asked himself a thousand times, should anyone wish to murder anything so exquisite?

They reached the first floor and, proceeding along the wide corridor off which the State Rooms opened, they came to the one which had been used by his grandmother.

Adam had designed it in the classical and impressive style for which he and his sons were to be famous.

There were damask panels set in the white walls, picked out in gold leaf. The bed, hung with curtains of pale blue silk, was supported by pillars of gold representing the trunks of a palm tree.

The canopy was surmounted by huge ostrich-feathered fronds and the Aubusson carpet was a riot of angels supporting garlands of pink roses tied with blue ribbons.

There were a number of windows in the room and one of them had been altered from the perfection of

Adam's symmetry so that it could open onto the balcony outside.

It was opposite the bed and as the Marquis set Idylla down gently against the pillows she could look out onto the large pots of azaleas, which decorated the balcony.

Above the marble balustrade there was the blue of the sky and below the sunshine glinted on water rising from a fountain in a wide stone basin filled with water lilies.

As the Marquis took his arms from Idylla Nurse bustled forward.

"If you'll go out onto the balcony for a moment, M'Lord," she said, "I'll get Miss Idylla into bed."

Obediently the Marquis walked across the room to pass through the French-windows.

He noted that there was a wicker-work chair with a foot-rest on the balcony and that there were iron struts attached to the back of the chair so that a muslin canopy could be added to protect the user from the sun.

He wished he could remember his grandmother, but she had in fact died before he was born.

He knew, however, that her diaries were in the Library, and he thought that he must find them and perhaps when she was better Idylla might like to read them.

He thought too that doubtless there would be people who would be surprised if not shocked that the chief State bed-room should be now occupied by a young woman about whom he knew nothing.

"You may come back now, M'Lord, if you wish."

The Marquis turned to see that Idylla was sitting up in the huge bed.

Now after what Nurse had said, he noted as he had

failed to do on previous visits, that she was wearing a thick cambric nightgown fastened high at the neck with plain bone buttons and with frills that fell over her small, thin, sensitive hands.

'Nurse's choice is certainly not mine!' he thought to himself.

Even so, Idylla looked strangely beautiful and he realised that her eyes were fixed on his with a somewhat worried expression in them.

"You are comfortable?" he asked gently.

"Thank you for bringing me .. here," Idylla said, "but it is .. too grand."

"Too grand?" the Marquis queried.

"You do not know who I am and, until you do, I feel it wrong that I should occupy a room that is so important."

"Nurse will tell you," the Marquis replied, "that no-one has used this room since my grandmother's time. But you will be able to sit out on the balcony and that will be like going into the garden until you are well enough actually to do so."

"When will .. that be?"

"Soon, very soon, I am sure."

"Suppose .. I never .. remember who I .. am?"

"You will remember," the Marquis answered reassuringly. "Concussion is a strange thing. Everything seems blank, then suddenly one becomes one's self again. It is like drawing up a blind and seeing the world outside."

There was a knock on the door. Nurse answered it and went from the room leaving the Marquis and Idylla alone.

"I want to .. ask you .. something."

He knew she was nervous.

"What is it?" he enquired.

She seemed to have difficulty in finding the words and because he felt that he might seem overwhelming towering above her, the Marquis sat down on the side of the bed.

"Tell me," he said with a smile that innumerable women had found irresistibly beguiling.

She looked at him and he saw that her blue eyes had become dark with worry.

'They are like the sea,' he thought, 'changing with the reflection of the sky, and now there is a cloud which obscures the light.'

"Tell me," he repeated softly.

"Do you .. believe that I .. am really .. a witch?"

Her voice was so low he could hardly hear the words.

"Nurse told you what happened?" he asked.

"She thought it might .. help me to .. remember."

"Then let me reassure you," the Marquis said. "I am absolutely convinced in my own mind that you are not a witch. Can you remember anything which happened before you were struck on the head with a blow that should have killed you?"

Idylla was still.

"No .. I cannot .. remember! I cannot remember it .. happening!" she whispered.

"You have no idea who it might be?"

"Why should anyone .. hate me so .. much?"

Her voice was very troubled and after a moment the Marquis said:

"Do not worry about it. Sooner or later everything will come back to you, as I have already said."

He knew she was listening and he went on:

"Memory is a strange thing. When one has had a

shock, merciful forgetfulness is sometimes Nature's way of protecting us from other damage."

"You mean .. mentally ?"

"That is what I am trying to say," the Marquis answered. "Whatever happened must have been terrifying and therefore you have forgotten at least temporarily the whole horror of it."

"I .. understand," she said simply.

"As for being a witch," the Marquis said with a smile, "I have never heard of a witch with blue eyes ! According to the books and all the local legends, they should be green !"

She gave a little sigh.

"I hope .. you are .. right."

"I know I am !"

"The maids are .. frightened of me," she said after a moment. "But then people round here are .. always frightened of .. witches !"

The Marquis waited.

He realised that what she had said implied that she not only remembered the past but also the part of the world in which she lived.

As if she realised what he was thinking she said :

"I .. I said 'round here', but I do not .. live here, do I ?"

"Where do you live ?" the Marquis asked.

She thought for a moment, then she made a helpless little gesture.

"I cannot .. remember ! It must have been .. somewhere where people .. talked of and were afraid of .. witches !"

"Does the County of Essex mean anything to you ?"

"Essex .. I seem to know the .. name. Is that .. where we are ?"

"Yes," he answered. "You are in Essex and the Blackwater River is to the north of us, the North Sea to the east and the River Crouch to the south."

"Blackwater .. the Blackwater River," Idylla repeated. "I know the .. name. I know .. I know it. But I cannot .. remember what it looks .. like. I want to .. remember .. but I .. cannot!"

"Let things come slowly," the Marquis advised. "As I have already told you, Idylla, Nature has her own way of healing, and I have the feeling that when the blow on your head has completely healed you will remember everything."

He spoke reassuringly, then Idylla's fingers were holding tightly onto his.

"If I do .. remember I am .. a witch," she said in a low voice, "you will not give me .. back to those .. people who Nurse said were trying to .. duck me in the .. water?"

"Look at me, Idylla!" the Marquis ordered.

She raised her worried eyes to his and he said quietly:

"I promise you, I swear it, if you want me to do so, that I would never inflict on anyone, man, woman or child, the cruelty and ignorance that expresses itself by persecuting those who have supposedly supernatural powers."

He continued slowly and impressively:

"There is really no such thing as a witch, Idylla, they do not exist, except in the imaginations of those who are too stupid and too uneducated to know better."

"You are .. sure of .. that?" Idylla asked hesitatingly after a moment.

"Quite sure!" the Marquis answered. "And I promise

98

you this as well. I will look after you and protect you. No-one will hurt you ever again."

He felt her fingers quiver on his and after a moment he said:

"Do you believe me?"

She was still looking up into his face, and as if what she saw in his grey eyes reassured her she said:

"I believe .. you."

Then she relinquished his hand.

"I think now you should rest," the Marquis said. "The more you rest and the more you sleep — and of course the more you take those magic potions that Nurse makes for you — the quicker you will get well."

There was a faint smile on Idylla's lips as she said:

"Nurse told me that you called her a witch."

"That is a joke as you know!" the Marquis replied. "But if we are going to pretend to believe in witches, then we have to believe in good ones as well as bad! Nanny is undoubtedly a good, benevolent fairytale witch, even though she may have a broom-stick hidden by the chimney-piece!"

Nurse had come into the room while the Marquis was speaking and she came towards the bed.

"Now, Your Lordship," she admonished, "don't go stuffing Miss Idylla's head with a lot of nonsensical notions before she remembers any sensible ones."

"I was just setting her mind at rest," the Marquis said, "and incidentally telling her that she must rest because that is the quickest way to get well."

"It is indeed," Nurse answered, "and she is going to sleep the moment she has had her luncheon."

The maid came in carrying a tray as she spoke and the Marquis turned towards the door.

"Good-bye, Idylla," he said, "and dream happy

dreams. There are a lot of people who could envy you for being able to forget the past."

She gave him a faint smile and he thought as he went downstairs he had spoken the truth.

It was the past that worried, upset and confused so many people.

What would it be like, he wondered, to start again from scratch, being already grown up, having nothing to regret, nothing to look back on and therefore obliged only to look forward?

It was a fascinating problem and he thought since he had come to the Castle there was no doubt that Idylla had brought a new interest into his life.

Not only was he absolutely determined to find out the truth about her and why anyone would wish to murder her, but also everything about her seemed to stimulate his brain and make him think on subjects he had never studied before. The mind was one.

How did the mind work as it did? Why was memory subject to physical injuries? Did Nature really erase horrors from the mind to save it from itself?

He considered various aspects of the subject as he ate an excellent luncheon. Then he left the Castle mounted on a fresh horse from the one on which he had ridden during the morning.

He had made up his mind during the night when he was thinking about Idylla that he would call at Trydell Hall and see if Sir Caspar was there.

If he was, the Marquis would try to find out if he had any knowledge of what had happened to Idylla, although he considered it unlikely that Sir Caspar would be able to help him.

Nevertheless Trydell Hall was nearer to the Druid stones than the Castle.

In fact they might almost be said to be on the Trydell Estate, although the piece of land on which they stood near the bank of the river was common land.

As the Marquis rode over the fields he was thinking of Caspar Trydell, and how he had been an unpleasant, tiresome little boy who had grown into a young man for whom he had what amounted to a dislike.

He was in fact much nearer the Marquis's age than his brother John had been, and it should have been natural for them to be friends. But Caspar had shown him an unaccountable hostility from the moment they first met.

Once when Caspar had come to the Castle in the company of his brother he had made himself so unpleasant, that the Marquis had never asked him again.

He thought now that perhaps the friendship John had accorded him might have been because he took the place of the brother with whom he had nothing in common.

Caspar was not physically strong and perhaps, because he resented his weakness, he expressed it by being rude and aggressive to nearly everyone with whom he came in contact.

There was no doubt that his father. Sir Harold, had disciplined him with unnecessary severity.

Extremely strict with both his sons he was a martinet at home, which John found trying as he grew older but Caspar resented with a sullenness that made him secretive and underhand.

Because he suspected that his father preferred his older brother to him, he waged a petty, ineffective, but nevertheless irritating vendetta against John.

He would hide his guns. He would move things he had put down in his bed-room or in one of the Sitting-Rooms. He once tried to hurt John's dog and received a punishment that made it quite certain he would never do such a thing again.

They were all petty actions, trivial in themselves, but carried on day after day, year after year, they created an atmosphere at the Hall which the Marquis sensed even though John never complained about his brother.

He only knew that where he himself was concerned he disliked Caspar and Caspar disliked him.

They therefore saw as little of each other as possible, but everything the Marquis had heard of Caspar in the years that followed only accentuated the distaste he had felt ever since he was a boy.

Riding now towards Trydell Hall he told himself that if he was to come frequently to stay at the Castle, it was important that he should make an attempt to be friendly with Caspar.

Their estates marched and there would obviously be a number of local difficulties and problems on which they would be forced to confer. It would be ridiculous to perpetuate childhood likes and dislikes when they were both grown men.

'If only John was here,' the Marquis thought with a sigh as he turned in at the great, impressive gates and rode up the avenue towards the house.

It was an ugly building with none of the artistic beauty of the Castle.

It had been built in the reign of Queen Anne and was square, red brick, with large windows but little else to recommend it.

The gardens, the Marquis noticed, were not well kept up and the house seemed somehow austere and forbidding. Moreover it was a long time before anyone came from the stables to take his horse.

Finally a groom appeared and the Marquis told him

to ring the bell before he dismounted and walked up the steps to the front door.

It was opened by an old man with grey hair, whose uniform hung loosely on him as if he had shrunk since it was made.

The Marquis looked at him for a moment, then he said:

"Good afternoon, Bates! It is Bates, is it not?"

"It is . ." the old man began, then exclaimed, peering at him with short-sighted eyes:

"Master Oswin! I never expected to see you here!"

"I am at the Castle," the Marquis explained. "I thought I would call on Sir Caspar."

"Sir Caspar's not here, Master . . I mean . . M'Lord." Bates replied. "But come in! Come in! It's a long time since you were last here, M'Lord."

"It is over ten years," the Marquis said. "I came over to spend Christmas with Mr. John."

"I remember, M'Lord," Bates said. "The Christmas of 1789 that were and Master John drowned the following summer."

The Marquis walked through the dark, oak-panelled Hall and into the room which opened out of it which, although it was called the Drawing-Room, had as Lady Trydell was dead, become more masculine year by year.

The elegant sofas and chairs had been replaced by larger and more comfortable ones, the *objets d'art* on the tables had gradually been removed to make way for books, tobacco-jars and pipe-stands.

There was however at the moment a very un-lived in look about the room and due, the Marquis thought, to Sir Harold being ill for some time before he died and doubtless being confined to his bed-room.

"How are you keeping, Bates?"

"Oh, well enough in myself, M'Lord, but I worry when I wonder what'll become of me."

"What do you mean by that?" the Marquis asked.

"Sir Caspar has dispensed with my services, M'Lord!"

"Dispensed with your services?" the Marquis exclaimed. "But, Bates, you have been here for years and I cannot imagine the place without you!"

"Fifty-three years, M'Lord! I came first when I was a boy of twelve and worked my way up until Sir Harold made me Butler."

"But why has Sir Caspar told you to go – and surely he has provided for you?"

"He's promised me a pension, M'Lord, but I doubts as I'll get it."

"And no cottage?" the Marquis asked sharply.

"None, M'Lord!"

The Marquis's lips tightened.

This confirmed all he had heard of Caspar Trydell and also what Roger Clarke had said.

"I cannot believe that is what Sir Caspar intends to do," he said and his voice was angry. "But if he does not give you a cottage, Bates, I promise you I will find you one, or else you can come to the Castle for as long as you wish to work."

The old man's face lit up.

"You mean that, M'Lord? I'm good for a few more years yet and if I've nothing to do I've a feeling 'twould be the quickest way to tumble into my grave. I've worked all me life and wouldn't know how to stop now."

"No, of course not, Bates, and I should be very glad to have you. I know how fond Mr. John was of you."

"Mr. John were a fine gentleman – none better!"

Bates said simply. "Everyone loved him. I can't think to this day how he come to drown as he did and him such a strong swimmer!"

"What did happen?" the Marquis asked. "I never came back to the Castle after his death, as you know. I joined the Army from Oxford and so I never heard the details."

"Mr. John went off swimming as he always did in the summer. You know, M'Lord, how he loved the water."

"I remember well," the Marquis answered.

"It was never too cold for Mr. John," Bates continued. "That particular day there was a sea-mist over the river and a full tide, but nothing like we have in the winter with a heavy swell. Nothing that would ordinarily have constituted any danger for Mr. John."

The Blackwater River was, as the Marquis well knew, tidal water. When a very high sea was running it could be considered dangerous, but in the summer there was no danger and John would have bathed from Steeple Creek.

"Mr. John never came back," Bates was saying, "and when it got late in the evening and near dinner-time I began to worry about him. I thought he might be late for the evening meal and that always annoyed Sir Harold. I asked Mr. Caspar if he had seen anything of Mr. John and he said no."

Bates sighed before he continued:

"Then it was dinner-time and Sir Harold said irritably that he would not wait for anyone. After dinner when there was still no sign of Mr. John I went to look for him myself and walked as far as the Creek."

Bates' voice expressed the anxiety he had felt.

"The fog had cleared and the tide had gone out," he went on. "I was just going home when I sees a towel and the robe and slippers Mr. John used to wear when he ran from the house to the Creek. As you know, M'Lord, it is nearly a mile, but it meant nothing to Mr. John. He was that fit!"

"No, of course not," the Marquis agreed.

"I went back and fetched two of the gardeners and several grooms, but by the time we got back to the water's edge it was dark and there was little we could do."

"When did anyone find him?" the Marquis asked.

"It were three days later," Bates replied with a tremor in his voice. "His body was swept up at Shingle Head Point. The tide must have carried him towards the sea, then somehow left his body behind on the other side of the river."

Bates stopped speaking, then he added:

"His head was badly injured, M'Lord, as if he had battered it against a sharp rock of some sort."

The Marquis was very still.

"Rock?" he queried. "But there are few rocks around this part of the world, Bates. It is mostly mud and sand."

"Yes, I know that, M'Lord. But it was a nasty wound on his head. The Undertakers had tidied him up a bit, but I could see it clearly."

The Marquis was silent for a moment, then he said:

"You thought it was done by a rock, Bates, but could the wound have been the result of having been hit with a weapon of some sort?"

"I don't think, M'Lord, that anyone would wish to harm Mr. John," Bates said quickly.

"I asked you a question," the Marquis persisted.

"I suppose it could, M'Lord. I never thought of it. Who'd want to hurt Mr. John? He was loved by everyone. There wasn't a man or boy on the estate who wouldn't have laid down his life for him. Very different to what they feels about Sir Caspar!"

As if he realised he was being indiscreet Bates looked over his shoulder as he spoke.

"When they found Mr. John," the Marquis went on, "how did they know who he was?"

"They didn't, M'Lord! Someone at Shingle Head Point reported there was a body on the beach, but as there was nothing anyone could do they took their time in notifying the Sheriff. He, of course, knew by then that Mr. John was missing."

"Who is the Sheriff?" the Marquis enquired. "And has he been changed since?"

"No, M'Lord. Colonel Trumble is still there. He hadn't been in office long when Mr. John was drowned."

"Where can I find him?" the Marquis asked.

"His office is in Chelmsford, M'Lord. But as it happens, he lives near Maldon, not more than ten miles from here I should imagine. Maldon Park the house is called and you'll find the Sheriff a very nice gentleman – very nice indeed!"

"Thank you, Bates," the Marquis said.

He slipped a guinea into the old man's hand and said:

"Now remember, the day you leave here we shall be delighted to see you at the Castle. I will instruct my agent, Mr. Clarke, that you will be arriving and everything will be prepared for you."

"Thank you, M'Lord! Thank you!"

There were tears in the old man's eyes as the Marquis walked across the hall.

"I forgot to tell you, M'Lord," Bates said as he reached the front door. "Sir Caspar may be returning this evening or to-morrow."

"He has gone to London?" the Marquis asked.

"Yes, M'Lord. He left the day before yesterday. He had some business to do."

As Bates spoke he involuntarily glanced up at the wall behind the Marquis who followed the direction of his eyes.

He saw that a large picture which had been one of the most valuable in Trydell Hall had gone. There was a mark on the wall where it had rested ever since the Marquis could remember.

Now he glanced round and saw that quite a number of the pictures painted of horses and dogs which had been Sir Harold's great joy had also disappeared.

It was quite obvious, he thought, what Sir Caspar's business in London would be.

Telling himself that his curiosity was justified he said to Bates in a quiet voice:

"I always thought Sir Harold was a wealthy man."

"That's what we all thought, M'Lord," Bates answered. "It is what Mr. Chiswick the Solicitor who came here after his death told me as an actual fact."

"Have you any idea of the wording of the Will?" the Marquis enquired.

"It may seem an impertinence, M'Lord, but having been with the family for so long I was naturally interested and Mr. Chiswick had known me for years."

Bates paused.

"He told me, M'Lord, exactly how Sir Harold had

left the Estate. He had not changed his Will since Mr. John was drowned."

The old man's voice quivered as he added:

"It's my belief, M'Lord, he couldn't bear to face the fact that Mr. John was no longer there."

"What did the Will say?" the Marquis persisted.

"Sir Harold's Will said," Bates recited, "To my eldest son, John, unconditionally, my entire Estate. In the event of his death, to any issue of the aforesaid John Trydell, also unconditionally, and without reserve."

"So there was no provision for Mr. Caspar!" the Marquis said slowly.

"There was, M'Lord, but only as an afterthought. As you know, Sir Harold never really liked Mr. Caspar and they did not get on, although he had no idea that anything might happen to Mr. John he had added a codicil."

"What was it?" the Marquis asked.

"In the event of my son John's death, and if he dies without issue, then the Estate shall pass to my second son, Caspar."

The Marquis was silent and Bates said:

"Mr. Chiswick told me, M'Lord, that Sir Harold was absolutely adamant against leaving anything to Mr. Caspar while Mr. John was alive.

" 'John will provide for his brother,' he said when the Solicitor pointed out to him that he was cutting his second son off without a penny. 'As far as I am concerned, he can live on his wits. It is the only asset he has anyway'."

Bates shook his head and added:

"Very bitter and nasty Sir Harold could be if anybody crossed him."

"And Mr. Caspar had crossed him?" the Marquis questioned.

"Time and time again, M'Lord. Not only did he ignore Sir Harold's advice, telling him he intended to live his own life, but he also came home to get his debts paid, not once but half a dozen times."

"And Sir Harold paid up?" the Marquis enquired.

"He said to me once after Mr. Caspar had rushed back to London with the money he had got out of him: 'I cannot see the family name dragged into the gutter, Bates, so what else can I do?'"

"I can understand his feelings," the Marquis said. "Thank you, Bates, I am glad to have had this talk with you."

The groom was waiting outside the door holding the Marquis's horse.

He swung himself into the saddle. As he rode back to the Castle he thought to himself he now had even more to think about than he had before.

5

Idylla was sitting on the balcony and the canopy over the wicker chair shaded her so that her face was in shadow.

She was wearing one of the new gowns that the Marquis had ordered for her from London. It was a soft pink, which made her eyes seem bluer than ever and brought out strange and unusual lights in her long hair.

It hung over her shoulders to below her small waist. Nurse had refused to allow her to pin it up on top of her head because the wound had not yet healed.

As the Marquis walked onto the balcony he thought that the huge pots of flame and white azaleas and the stone balustrade were a perfect setting for her.

It was almost as if she toned in with the house and became a part of it, even though he still thought of her as a nymph rising from deep water.

She smiled at him spontaneously and it illuminated her face and seemed to echo in her eyes.

"How are you to-day?" he asked.

"So much better that I would like to go out into the garden," Idylla replied, "but Nurse will not let me."

"It is no use arguing with Nanny, as I have found all my life," the Marquis replied. "She always gets her own way!"

"But I want to see your garden," Idylla protested. "The flowers look so lovely from here, but they are so far away."

"To-morrow, the next day or the day after, you will be able to touch them and pick them if you wish to do so," the Marquis promised, "but there is no hurry."

"N . no . . I suppose not," Idylla said hesitatingly, "but I . . might not . . be here."

"Why should you say that?" the Marquis enquired.

She looked back through the open window into the bed-room and saw that when the Marquis appeared Nurse had left the room.

The Marquis was aware that her expression was troubled and after a moment he asked gently:

"What is worrying you?"

He pulled up a chair to sit facing her as he spoke, his back to the garden.

She looked down at her hands and twisted her long fingers together as if she was agitated.

"Try to tell me what is troubling you," the Marquis insisted.

The scratch marks had almost completely gone from her face, but there were still some visible on her arms.

Her gown was short-sleeved, but she wore a long floating scarf which covered her shoulders and hid some of the marks.

"You will . . think I am very . . foolish," she said in a low voice.

"I cannot promise you I will not think so, until you tell me what this is all about," the Marquis said. "But I think it unlikely that anything you say would seem foolish to me at any rate."

There was a note of sincerity in his voice which seemed to reassure Idylla and after a moment she said:

"I . . I want you to give me . . something."

"What is it?" the Marquis enquired.

"A cross."

He looked at her in astonishment.

Women had asked him for a great many things in his life, but no-one until now had requested a cross!

"Why?" he asked.

"It is difficult to . . explain," Idylla said. "Perhaps I am in fact a . . witch . . at any rate I have a strong and inescapable . . feeling of . . evil around me!"

The Marquis bent forward in his chair, his arms on his knees.

"Explain to me exactly what you mean by that."

"It is difficult to put into words," Idylla answered, "but it is there. There is evil approaching me . . reaching out . . towards me. It is dark . . horrible and I feel it is . . impossible for me to . . escape."

"When do you feel this?"

"Mostly at night, and in the day-time if I am . . alone."

"Do you think a cross would keep it away from you?"

"Someone once told me so . . but I cannot remember who it was. I have been trying . . trying desperately hard to recall what was said . . but all I know is that I . . must have a . . cross."

She paused, then said:

"I remember my prayers . . I remember all of them and I say them when the . . evil is . . there and sometimes it . . helps."

"Not always?" the Marquis enquired.

"Nearly always . . and if I pray hard enough. But when I am asleep it is difficult . . then I can feel it coming . . nearer!"

There was a tremor in her voice and he knew she was really frightened.

He put out his hand and laid it on hers.

"I will get you a cross," he promised, "but I cannot help thinking that this is just imagination."

"I thought . . that too."

"You are sensible enough to realise that after having received a blow on the head causing a tremendous shock to the system, it is easy being weak and listless to be mentally depressed also."

"I have told myself that over and over again," Idylla said, "but the . . evil is still there . . almost as if it was trying to take . . possession of . . me."

Two weeks ago, the Marquis thought, he would have laughed such a suggestion to scorn. But since he had come to the Castle and had heard so much about magic and witchcraft he could not help feeling the whole thing could not be shrugged off merely as the superstitions of ignorant peasants.

He had found some books in the Library, as he had expected to do, which dealt with the subject.

Among them he read the contention of Sir William Blackstone, Vinerian Professor of English Law at Oxford University in the 18th century.

"to deny the possibility, nay actual existence of witchcraft, is flatly to contradict the revealed word of God, and various passages both of the Old and New Testaments."

Sir William then went on to quote from a number of passages in the Bible, starting from Exodus, where it said :

"Thou shalt not suffer a witch to live."

From another book the Marquis learnt that in 1563 Queen Elizabeth had passed an Act against enchantments and witchcrafts, which began by saying:

". . . if any person or persons after the said first day of June shall use, practise, or exercise any witchcraft, enchantment, charm or sorcery . . ."

Until the 13th century witchcraft was regarded as a Christian heresy and the *Canon Episcopal* was the first to present this view in writing:

"*Some wicked women, reverting to Satan, and seduced by the illusions and phantasms of demons, believe and profess that they can ride at night with Diana on certain beasts . . .*"

Again Sir Thomas Browne in his *Religio Medici* wrote in 1643:

"*For my part, I have ever believed and do now know, that there are Witches.*"

It was obvious, the Marquis deduced, that a belief in witchcraft had been common in the days of Christ, and the violence with which the Catholic Church, and after the Reformation the Protestants, persecuted witches and sorcerers was to admit that such a heresy existed.

How, he asked himself now, could it be possible that this young girl, apart from the terrible ordeal she had gone through of which thankfully she had no memory, should be aware of evil if she had never come in contact with it before?

Because he did not speak Idylla looked up at him fearfully.

"I said you would .. think me .. foolish," she said.

"I think nothing of the sort!" the Marquis replied.

"I was merely considering what this feeling could be and what caused it."

"I do not feel it now because .. you are here," Idylla said, "and never when Nanny is with me. It is when I am .. alone."

"Would you like to have someone to sleep in your room?" the Marquis asked. "I know Nanny would agree if I suggest a bed should be put up for her beside yours."

"No, no!" Idylla said quickly. "All I want is a cross. I know that will keep me safe."

"How do you know that?" the Marquis enquired.

He knew that to invoke the name of God and to confront the Devil with the symbol of the cross was according to the books on magic, to confound him. But he was interested to know how Idylla was aware of it.

"I think I must always have known," she answered slowly, "that good can overcome evil and those who believe in God can remain unharmed by the Devil. It is just that I have never had to apply such beliefs to .. myself until .. now."

"But those beliefs were there? Someone taught you the truth?" the Marquis persisted.

"Someone must have," she agreed looking a little bewildered. "But .. who was .. it?"

"Can you remember your mother?"

"I am not .. sure."

"Your father?"

She shook her head decisively.

"You will remember in time," the Marquis said his fingers tightening over hers. "Let it come naturally. I will bring you a cross and you must go on saying your prayers."

"I always say them," she answered. "I thank God too

that you saved me. If you had not come I would have
. . died in the water."

"Do not think about it," the Marquis urged.

"Perhaps it is their . . hatred I still feel," Idylla said
as if she was speaking to herself.

She looked down at her arms as she spoke; the
scratches were healing but the bruises which had been
black and blue were now pale orange and yellow. They
were still vivid against the whiteness of her skin.

"I am grateful . . very grateful," she said. "And I
have no right to . . complain. Those people might have
. . broken my legs or my arms. They might have . .
blinded me !"

"I told you not to think of such things," the Marquis
said with a sharp note in his voice.

He paused, then said :

"I am going to prescribe a remedy of my own to
sweep away the depression which I am sure comes
merely from loneliness."

"What is . . that ?" Idylla asked.

"I am inviting you to dine with me to-night," the Marquis said. "I am sure Nanny will not allow you to go
downstairs, so we shall have dinner in the *boudoir*
which opens off your bed-room. Have you seen it yet ?"

"I peeped inside," Idylla confessed. "It is a very lovely
room !"

"Then that is where we will dine," the Marquis said,
"and perhaps you will wear one of the pretty gowns
that came from London."

"Some more arrived this morning," Idylla said, "and
I have not yet thanked you for them. How could I be so
remiss ?"

She looked so conscience-stricken that the Marquis
smiled.

"You may thank me by looking particularly pretty to-night," he said. "Like you I am finding it rather lonely at the Castle, at least at meal-times, so it will be a treat for both of us."

"Am I keeping you .. here when you should be in London with your .. friends?" Idylla asked in a low voice.

"You are one of the reasons for my staying," the Marquis agreed. "But I assure you it is no hardship. I am trying to solve a mystery — your mystery, Idylla — and I am finding it extremely intriguing."

He thought the same when later in the afternoon he drew the stallion he was riding to a standstill beside the Druid stones.

Standing well above the river on a piece of high ground they were, the Marquis thought, quite obviously a landmark, and he was in fact convinced in his own mind they had no religious significance of any sort.

It was however difficult to imagine how they got there.

Even if they had been brought up the Blackwater River by boat it would have required an army of men to drag them over the sand and up the crumbling side of the river bank to the ground above it.

Granted the river might have altered its course and it would have been easier at high tide, but even so the stones were enormous and of a type of granite which the Marquis did not recognise.

There were only three of them, which again made him think they were unlikely to have been used by the Druids.

Two of them stood over 6′ high and the one between them was horizontal which made the local inhabitants sure it had been used as an altar.

There were still bloodstains on the side of this stone, which the Marquis knew had come from the cock which had been left on Idylla's unconscious body.

"Who could have put her there?" he asked himself again, "and why, having murdered her, as he thought, should he have bothered to kill a cock and place it on her?"

There seemed to be no possible answer to his questions!

He was staring at the stones with such concentration that he started when he heard a voice beside him say:

"Excuse me, M'Lord."

He looked down and saw a middle-aged man whose face was definitely familiar.

He was dressed roughly but not in the smock of a farm-labourer. His coat had the deep side-pockets of those usually worn by game-keepers.

"Pulsey!" the Marquis exclaimed. "I thought I recognised you!"

"That's right, M'Lord. I used to take ye and Mr. John shooting in th' old days when ye were living up at th' Castle."

"You heard I was back?" the Marquis asked.

"Everyone knows that, M'Lord, and I hopes for a chance of a word with Your Lordship."

"What can I do for you, Pulsey?"

"I wondered if there be any sort of job at th' Castle, M'lord. I'd do anything. I'm not proud."

"You are no longer employed by Sir Caspar?"

"No, M'Lord! He sacked me three year ago."

"And why was that?"

" 'Twas after his accident, M'Lord. He'd no use for a game-keeper when that had happened."

"I had not heard of any accident," the Marquis said.

"Well, 'twere not exactly an accident, M'Lord, but Sir Caspar lost the first finger o' his right hand. It were amputated up to th' third joint."

"Why was that?" the Marquis enquired.

"He fell off his horse onto a bit o' broken glass. He thought 'twas only a cut, but some poison got into it and th' doctors in Chelmsford said that amputation was the only way to save his arm."

"That was unfortunate."

"Of course, M'Lord, there be them who said it be witchcraft!"

"Witchcraft?" the Marquis repeated sharply. "How was that?"

"I shouldn't be repeating local gossip, M'Lord."

"I am interested. Tell me what was said."

The Marquis had a feeling that indirectly Pulsey was warning him as he said:

"Sir Caspar were interested, as you might put it, M'Lord, in a girl living in Latchingdon who'd come from th' Witch-Country."

The Marquis could not help thinking that every conversation he held seemed to come back by some way or another to witchcraft.

"Go on!"

"Her were a decent girl, although there be stories about her aunt with whom she be staying, some people saying her be a witch!"

"What happened?" the Marquis enquired.

"Mr. Caspar, for Sir Harold was alive in those days, went after her, an' her aunt turned him out o' th' house. 'Lay one finger on my niece,' the neighbours heard her say, 'an' your arm'll wither away and ye'll have no more use in it!' Very ferocious her were by all accounts."

"And it was shortly after this that Sir Caspar lost his finger?" the Marquis asked.

"A week later, M'Lord! Th' people in these parts took it as a warning, an' from all accounts Mr. Caspar took it as a warning as well!"

"You mean he did not go near the girl again?"

"No, M'Lord. But he took against witches, so to speak. Encouraged the persecution of 'em so 'tis said, an' reported some of the old women around here to th' Magistrates so that they were taken to Chelmsford for investigation."

The Marquis was listening intently.

A new idea had come into his mind which had not been there before.

He was silent and after a moment Pulsey said awkwardly:

"I hopes I did no wrong in atelling Your Lordship these things. Ye lived around here as a boy and ye knows how they talks in villages."

"I do indeed," the Marquis said slowly. "Come up to the Castle to-morrow, Pulsey. I will speak to Mr. Clarke and see if we can find you something to do."

The man's eyes seemed to light up.

"If you'd do that, M'Lord, it'd be a real kindness."

"I do not forget old friends, Pulsey," the Marquis said. "And you gave Mr. John and me some grand days in the past."

"Aye, that's true, M'Lord. D'ye remember th' time when ye brought down two teal with one shot?"

"I do indeed!" the Marquis laughed.

They reminisced for a little while as sportsmen always will, each trying to cap the other's memory.

When the Marquis rode back to the Castle, it seemed to him that a new line of thought was opening up in front of him and it led more and more directly to Caspar Trydell!

He was however determined first that Idylla's dinner-party should be a success.

He ordered the room to be decorated with flowers and chose the menu with care.

He took the same trouble over his clothes that he would have done had he been dining at Carlton House.

It was difficult to think that any man could look more magnificent than the Marquis in a deep blue satin coat and a white frilled cravat that had been starched to exactly the right stiffness.

He wore no jewellery, which was Beau Brummell's most inexorable dictum for a gentleman, but when he entered the Sitting-Room which had been his grand-mother's *boudoir* he carried in his hand a small velvet-covered jewel-box.

Idylla was already waiting for him, sitting on a *chaise longue*, her feet covered with a satin-rug.

"She may dine with you, M'Lord," Nurse had said, "but she will rest at the same time or I'll not be respons-ible for her any longer. It's too soon for her to be getting up and doing things, when her memory's as lost as Mrs. Darwin's husband who ran off to sea twenty years ago and has never been heard of since!"

The Marquis laughed.

"It will do your patient no harm to eat with me rather than alone in bed," he·said. "I will not keep her up late, that I promise you!"

He thought that Nurse was unconvinced and added in the joking tone that she always found irresistible:

"Come on, Nanny! Do not be a spoil-sport! You were young yourself once, and you know as well as I do that Miss Idylla, with her looks, should be the Toast of St.

James's rather than having nothing more intoxicating then your herbal potions!"

"They're much better for her and would be for you too, M'Lord, than those wines that you and His Royal Highness imbibe far too freely!"

"What do you know about it, Nanny?" the Marquis enquired. "Unless of course you fly off on your broomstick to listen down the chimney to our carousing, or turn yourself into a fly upon the wall!"

"Get along with you, Your Lordship!" Nanny said. "If you talk like that you'll have the rest of the household refusing to obey my orders. It's bad enough now to have the young ones running away when they see me coming!"

"Shall I tell them firmly and categorically once and for all that you are a witch?" the Marquis teased.

"There's no such things as witches!" Nanny said. "And as for that poor child, she's more of an angel than a witch, and that's the truth!"

There was no doubt that Idylla did look very lovely wearing a gown that was made of gauze embroidered with silver.

It shimmered with every movement and the Marquis thought that she might have been dressed in moonlight.

As a concession to the importance of the occasion Nanny had allowed her to arrange her hair but only at the back of her head and not on top of it.

A coil however became her and made her face seem smaller and more spiritual than when framed by the long dark tresses.

Her blue eyes seemed to the Marquis the colour of the Madonna's robe, and they were sparkling with excitement as he came across the room to her.

"You do look magnificent!" she said spontaneously

as he reached her side. "Do you dress like that when you go to Carlton House?"

"At times I add a few decorations," the Marquis replied. "Then I sparkle even more than you will when you wear what I have brought you."

He put the jewel-case into her hand. She took it from him, then looked up to ask:

"What is it?"

"It is what you asked me for," the Marquis answered, "a cross."

She opened the jewel-case and gave a little exclamation of surprise.

Among his grandmother's jewellery, some of which had been left in the Castle after she died, the Marquis had found a cross.

It was set with large diamonds and could be worn as a pendant with a chain which was interspersed with small pearls.

It was a beautiful piece of jewellery and, as he had expected, Idylla stared at it spellbound before she said in a low voice:

"I cannot take .. this from you! It is too .. grand and far too . valuable!"

"It is a cross, Idylla, and the only one I can find at the moment. It belonged to my grandmother and I feel sure she would like you to wear it."

Idylla hesitated for a moment, then she said:

"May I have it as a .. loan then when I leave .. here I can give it back to you?"

"Shall we agree you will wear it until it is no longer necessary?" the Marquis asked. "Let me put it on for you."

He sat down on the edge of the *chaise longue* on which she was sitting and took the cross and chain from the velvet box. Undoing the clasp he held the necklace in both his hands so that he could encircle her neck.

She turned her head to one side so that he could see to fasten the clasp underneath the heavy coil of her hair. Then as he removed his hand she put up her own to hold the cross and look down at it.

"It is lovely! The most beautiful piece of jewellery I have ever seen!" she cried. "Thank you more than I can possibly say! I know I shall feel safe now. Thank you!"

She lifted her face as she spoke like a child and the Marquis realised she intended to kiss his cheek in a spontaneous act of gratitude.

He did not move and he felt her lips soft and warm against his skin. It gave him a strange feeling to which he could not put a name.

Then as the door opened and the footmen came into the room bringing the first dishes for dinner he rose to his feet.

The table was placed in front of the *chaise longue* and Newman had seen that it was exactly the right height.

There was a comfortable high backed chair for the Marquis and beside the table there was the large crested bucket filled with ice in which rested several bottles of wine.

There were gold candelabra to hold the lighted candles and there were small white orchids as a decoration.

"I like orchids," Idylla said, "but they have no smell."

"I noticed when I put the cross round your neck," the Marquis said, "that your hair held the fragrance of lilies of the valley."

"My favourite flower," Idylla told him. "So Nurse distilled some of their perfume for me."

She smiled as she added shyly :

"I am so glad you .. liked it .. but I felt it was .. cruel to have to spoil so many lovely blooms."

"I think they would be willing to die for you!" the Marquis said quietly, and she blushed.

The dinner was delicious. Idylla took only tiny portions of each course and sipped the wine a little tentatively, but the Marquis knew she was enjoying herself.

"Even though my memory has gone," she said, "I am sure that this is the first time I have ever had such a delicious dinner or dined with anyone so distinguished!"

"Can you be sure of that?" the Marquis enquired.

"I am quite, quite sure that I have never met anyone like you," she replied.

She had spoken with an unaffected ease, but now her blue eyes met the Marquis's and quite unexpectedly there was a constraint between them.

It was something neither of them could have explained, but it was as if it was hard to go on talking and difficult to take their eyes from each other.

They had both been laughing and discussing a number of subjects but suddenly there was no need for words.

The footmen took away the last of the dishes, then removed the table.

Newman brought up an arm-chair and set it beside Idylla's *chaise longue*. He placed a cut-glass decanter of brandy beside it on a small side-table, then withdrew from the room.

They were alone and Idylla's eyes dropped as if she was shy, and she put her fingers to touch the cross to make sure it was still there.

The Marquis watched her for a few moments, then he said:

"You are very beautiful, Idylla!"

Her eyes were raised to his in astonishment.

"Beautiful?" she questioned. "No-one has ever told me that before!"

"How do you know?" the Marquis enquired.

"If they had, I am sure I would have .. remembered."

"Is it so important?"

"Very important! I .. I want you to think me .. beautiful."

"Why?" the Marquis asked.

The question seemed to confuse her a little.

"You have been so .. kind," she murmured. "You have given me .. lovely gowns and lent me this .. diamond cross to .. wear."

She paused and as if she thought this was inadequate she added:

"You also saved me from .. dying and brought me to your .. house."

"And so for these reasons and these reasons alone you want me to think you beautiful?" the Marquis asked.

There was silence. Then after a moment Idylla said hesitatingly:

"Nanny has told me of the smart and important people whom you know in London and the many .. lovely ladies you .. entertain. I did not want you to be .. disappointed in me."

"Shall I tell you," the Marquis asked, "that not only am I not disappointed, but I have never entertained anyone as lovely as you, Idylla, and that is the truth!"

Her eyes seemed to be full of stars.

"Do you .. mean that?"

"I mean it very sincerely."

The Marquis set down his glass of brandy on the table beside him and rose from the arm-chair to sit, as he had done earlier in the evening, on the side of Idylla's *chaise longue*.

It was quite wide and she was so slight and slim that there was plenty of room for him.

At the same time they were very close to each other and he knew that a little tremor ran through her although he was sure it was not from fear.

"Before dinner," he said in his deep voice, "when I gave you the diamond cross you kissed my cheek when you thanked me. I want to thank you, Idylla, for one of the most enchanting evenings I have ever spent. May I do that?"

He drew a little nearer to her as he spoke. As she did not answer he put his arm behind her and drew her towards him.

Just for a moment he looked down into her blue eyes, then slowly his mouth sought hers.

It was a very gentle kiss as if the Marquis was afraid to frighten her. Her lips were sweet and soft as the petals of a flower and as pure and untouched.

There was something inexpressibly lovely in her innocence that the Marquis had never found before. Then he raised his head and laid her back gently against the cushions.

She looked at him with her blue eyes that were no longer shining like stars but seemed to him to be filled with the softness and mystery of the moonlight.

"I thought a .. kiss would be .. like that," she murmured almost beneath her breath.

"Like what?" the Marquis asked.

"So perfect .. like flying into the .. sky .. and like a .. prayer."

"A prayer?" the Marquis asked puzzled.

"Sometimes when I am praying," Idylla explained, "I feel as if I am with the angels .. I can hear them singing and share their .. exaltation. That is what I felt .. just now when you .. kissed me."

The Marquis drew in his breath.

Lifting her hand he kissed first the back of it, then turning it over his lips lingered for a moment on the softness of her palm.

"There are so many things we have to say to each other, Idylla," he said. "But not to-night. I do not want to tire you. I want you to go to sleep thinking of the kiss we have just given each other and the cross round your neck which will keep you safe."

He kissed her hand again, then rose to his feet.

"Good-night, Idylla," he said softly. "You are correctly named. You are perfection!"

There was a note in his voice that made Idylla vibrate to it as if it were the music of angels. Then he was gone from the room and Nurse came bustling in like a strong wind from the sea.

"It's half after nine o'clock," she said, "and time you were in bed an hour ago. I told His Lordship not to keep you up late. If you are tired to-morrow, don't blame me!"

Idylla did not answer. She only knew as Nanny undressed her, chattering all the time, that her happiness could only have come from Heaven itself.

.   .   .   .   .   .

The Marquis awoke and realised he had been asleep after lying awake for a long time.

He had gone to bed just before midnight not because

he was tired, but because he knew his valet was waiting up for him.

Surprisingly, although he was not usually concerned with his servants' feelings, he had thought that Harris might be tired.

It was a warm night and the windows of his room were wide open. He had lain feeling the breeze blowing through the curtains and thought the softness of it was like the touch of Idylla's lips.

He knew that what he felt when he had kissed her was quite different from anything he had known before.

It was difficult to count how many women he had kissed in his life, but it was somehow an indictment against himself to realise that the majority of kisses he had given and received had meant absolutely nothing. He could not now even remember them.

Looking back he found somewhat to his consternation that few women, once he had parted from them, had left a lasting impression upon his mind.

They had been beautiful, captivating, and they had entertained him at the time with an expertise which had made him believe that each in her turn was unique and meant more to him than any woman had meant before.

But always such ideas had proved to be illusory.

Sooner or later he had acknowledged to himself that they no longer interested him and that their allurements had worn thin or vanished altogether.

"What do I feel for Idylla?" he asked, and told himself it was impossible that she could really mean more and seem so utterly different from anyone he had known in the past.

After all she was very much younger than he was and

much younger also than the women who had attracted him over the years.

He had thought that he only liked sophistication.

It had certainly been easier to have a love-affair with a woman who was versed in not only the tricks and allurements of love but also in the etiquette which the Marquis had always believed turned love-making into an Art.

Idylla was innocent of all these things, and he had known when he kissed her that she responded to his kiss not only with her lips but with some spirituality that he had not expected.

She had tried to explain it to him, but he had recognised it even before she put it into words.

Strangely enough what she had felt had been what he had felt himself.

"Dammit!" he said in the darkness of his room. "This is magic!"

He spoke aloud and as he did so knew he was trying to sweep away the enchantment simply because he could not explain it and was almost afraid of it.

It was a nonsensical idea, and he tried to tell himself that because this was a district of sorcery and unenlightenment he had merely been caught in the toils of witchcraft to the point where he had begun to believe in it.

And yet however much the cynical part of his mind tried to refute it, when he had kissed Idylla it *had* been different!

He knew that nothing he could think or say could change the fact that she had aroused in him a strange emotion such as he had never known before.

He had fallen asleep to dream of her, and yet now for no apparent reason he was awake.

The wind was still moving the curtains but it was noiseless. He wondered why he felt so alert when he was sure it was not yet dawn.

He had a strange feeling that Idylla had called him. But even if she had done so, he could not have heard her in his room which, although it was on the same floor, was two large State Rooms away.

Again he had the feeling that she was calling out to him.

"This place is making me imagine things!" he said to himself. "The sooner I go back to civilisation the better!"

Nevertheless he got out of bed, put on his robe and slippers before he walked to the window to look out at the night.

As he had expected the sky was filled with stars and the moon was overhead.

It was a young moon, little more than a crescent, and it made him think of the shimmer of Idylla's gown as he had looked at her across the table at dinner.

At the thought of her, he glanced along the side of the house in the direction of her room, then froze into immobility.

He could see the balcony which had been built for his grandmother standing out sharply against the Adam façade, and standing on it quite distinct in the light from the stars there was a man!

The Marquis stared in astonishment, then saw there was another man in the garden below and suspended between the balcony and the ground there was a figure in white.

For a moment he could not imagine what was happening or what the men could be doing. Then in a flash he

realised they were conveying a body, and it must be
Idylla!

For an instant the Marquis felt as if he was frozen
into immobility with the surprise of it. Then running
across the room and pulling open the door he turned not
towards Idylla's room, but towards the stairs.

Some part of his brain which had been trained for
immediate action in the Army told him clearly, almost
as if it were an order, that to prevent effectively what
was happening he must attack from the ground.

He had never realised before how high the staircase
was or what a long way it was across the Hall and
down the passage which led to the Sitting Room which
lay beneath Idylla's bed-room.

As he went, running quicker than he had run since
he was a boy, the Marquis calculated that he would
have to open the window and climb out onto the terrace.

He could approach from another angle but he thought
to himself that the man who was waiting to take hold
of Idylla as she was lowered down to him would be
looking upwards.

The Marquis opened the door of the room quietly and
made no attempt to draw the curtains back but slipped
behind them.

Through the glass in the window he could see the
man quite clearly and his head was tipped back.

Now the Marquis could see that there was a ladder
up which the first man must have climbed and down
which they were sliding Idylla to the ground.

The windows of the Castle were kept well oiled and
the Marquis was able to turn the latch and open the
casement without making a sound.

Then he turned back into the room and picked up a
candlestick from a side-table near the window.

It was made of heavy silver and the square base with its pointed corners made it a formidable weapon.

Clasping it firmly in his right hand he slipped over the sill and out onto the terrace, only slightly incommoded by his long silk robe.

Now the Marquis saw that Idylla was only a foot from the ground and that her body made it quite impossible for the man who was holding onto her to see his approach.

The Marquis also imagined that the other man who had let Idylla down from the balcony would now be climbing down himself.

Swiftly and silently he moved, nearer and nearer, and before the man could even turn towards him he raised the candlestick and hit him hard on the side of the head.

The man gave a little cry and fell to the ground. As he did so the man on the ladder jumped at the Marquis.

He was a large man, and had he landed as he intended on the Marquis's back he would have felled him.

As it was the Marquis stepped aside at exactly the right moment and the man sprawled forward, his arms outstretched to save himself. As he did so the Marquis brought the silver candlestick down hard on the back of his head.

He fell forward as if pole-axed.

The Marquis threw the candlestick down beside him and turned to Idylla.

She was standing propped against the ladder and he saw that she had been gagged and bound with a rope which encircled her so that from her shoulders to her ankles she was unable to move.

He took off the gag and she gave a little cry of fear and hid her face against his shoulder.

"It is all right, my darling! You are safe! They have not hurt you?"

She was unable to answer him but he could feel her trembling as with his free hand he endeavoured to undo the rope which had been wound tightly round her body.

Finally the ropes dropped to the ground and without even looking at the men he had felled, the Marquis picked Idylla up in his arms and carried her to the window out of which he had climbed.

"This is going to be rather difficult," he said gently, "but it will take far longer to go round to the front door and try to arouse the staff."

She raised her head from his shoulder at his words and he lifted her very gently through the window onto the floor inside.

"Hold onto a chair or anything which will prevent you from falling while I climb in beside you," he said.

The calm, unhurried way in which he spoke made her obey him even while he was aware that she was still trembling violently.

He had released her only for a very few seconds before he too was in the room. He picked her up and held her close against him.

"You are safe and I am taking you up to bed," he said

She was wearing only a thin, diaphanous nightgown which he had ordered for her from London and he could feel that her body was very cold and shaking with fear as he carried her up the stairs and back to her bedroom.

He set her down on the bed and saw that the sheets had been pulled back and tumbled by the men who had tried to abduct her.

As he laid her down against the pillows he saw in

the dim light coming through the window, the glitter of the cross which she wore round her neck and thought that it must have protected her.

Her hands were clinging to him and he said gently:

"Listen, my darling, I am going to leave you for just a few minutes while I rouse the night-watchman and have these scoundrels who were trying to kidnap you tied up and put into a safe place. Would you like me to call Nanny? Or will you wait for me to return to you?"

He saw she could not speak and went on:

"I will be as quick as I can. I want to hear what happened. I want to reassure you that it will not happen again, and in case you are apprehensive I am going to shut the window onto the balcony and lock it."

He moved across the room as he spoke. When he had locked the window he lit the candlebra holding three candles which stood by her bed and looked down at her.

He thought in the golden glow of the candlelight she did not look as fearful as he might have expected.

"You will be all right?" he asked.

"I prayed you would .. save me," she whispered.

"I heard your prayer," the Marquis answered simply.

Idylla gave a sudden cry.

"I .. remember! Now .. I remember .. and I know .. who .. I am!"

6

It only took the Marquis a few minutes to find the night-watchmen, instruct them to awaken Newman and several footmen, and bring the two men he had left unconscious into the house.

He ordered that they were to be bound and locked up until the morning when he would send for the Sheriff and also interrogate them himself.

As he hurried back to Idylla's bed-room he thought now that it seemed foolish that while there were night-watchmen inside the Castle, no-one had ever thought it necessary to patrol the grounds.

"Who could have imagined," he asked himself, "that anyone would wish to abduct a guest?"

It seemed incredible that not only had an attempt been made to kidnap Idylla, but it would also have been successful if by some strange, almost supernatural perception, the Marquis had not become aware of it in time to save her.

He entered her bed-room to see by the light of the candles that she was leaning back against the pillows, but at the same time her eyes were watching the door for his return.

He had deliberately not awakened Nurse, although he thought perhaps he ought to do so, because he wished to be alone with Idylla and hear what she had to tell him.

He was sure too that he would be able to deal with her shock and fear better than anyone else.

He crossed the room to sit down beside the bed and instinctively her hands went out to him.

He could feel her fingers very cold and trembling in his, and he knew she must be exerting great self-control not to be hysterical after what had occurred.

"I remember . . who I . . am," she said in a low, hesitating voice.

"I want to hear everything," the Marquis said soothingly. "But first, because there is no hurry and we have the whole night in front of us, I am going to light the fire because I know you are cold and ask you if there is anything you would like to drink."

He smiled as he said :

"I feel Nanny, if we woke her, would insist on that."

"There is . . some of her . . lemonade with honey in it on the . . side-table," Idylla said.

The Marquis realised again that she was making a tremendous effort to speak normally.

"I will fetch it and now try to relax and realise that it is all over and you are safe !"

He smiled at her beguilingly, then went to the fireplace where the fire was laid. He found a taper on the mantelshelf which he lit from the candles by the bed.

The flames sprang up over the dry wood and then the Marquis found the lemonade on the side-table as Idylla had said, and poured her out a glass.

"I feel really you ought to have something hot and sweet," he said. "Is that not always the prescription after shock ?"

She did not reply but took the glass from him, Although her hands were shaking she managed to drink a little before he set it down for her on the table by the bed.

"Now tell me first what happened here," he said.

She reached out towards his hand and he took her fingers in his warm grasp and thought that no-one could look more beautiful after passing through such a frightening ordeal.

"I must .. have been .. sound asleep," she began in a voice that quivered, "because when I .. awoke it was to find the two .. men standing by the bed. One of them tied a .. handkerchief over my mouth."

It was easy to see in her eyes what a shock it had been.

"I tried to .. struggle," she went on, "but I think .. actually I was too .. terrified to .. move."

She made a sound that was like a sob before she went on :

"They .. wound the .. rope around me and what made it so .. horrible was that they .. never spoke. I kept .. telling myself it was a .. nightmare and I would .. wake up."

The Marquis's fingers tightened on hers.

"I know what happened then," he said. "They carried you to the balcony and started to slide you down the ladder by another rope which they had attached to your waist."

"Yes .. that is right. It was .. then that I began praying .. I felt .. somehow that I could .. reach you and tell .. you what was .. happening to me."

"I did hear you," the Marquis said. "Your prayer awakened me."

"I .. felt it .. must," Idylla said. "I .. needed you so .. desperately !"

"I think if I had not heard you but found your bed empty in the morning, I would have gone mad!" the Marquis said.

There was a note in his voice which sounded raw even to himself, and he added more lightly:

"Or perhaps I should then have been quite certain that you were a witch and had flown away on your broomstick!"

Idylla tried to smile as he meant her to do, but failed.

"Now your memory has come back?" the Marquis asked very gently.

"It was .. when I saw you .. hit the man who was .. holding me," Idylla said hesitatingly. "Something seemed to .. clear in my mind .. and when you hit the .. other man .. I knew!"

"What did you know?"

"That it had .. happened .. before. That I had .. seen a man hit .. Grandpapa in .. such a manner!"

Her last words were indistinct and now the Marquis saw the tears come into her eyes. With a convulsive gesture she moved towards him so that she could cry against his shoulder.

He held her very closely as she cried with sobs that shook her whole body.

He could feel her trembling beneath the soft lawn of her nightgown and as he kissed her hair there was the fragrance of lilies-of-the-valley.

"It is all right, my precious, my darling!" he said. "Please do not cry like that. I cannot bear it!"

He felt her stiffen and knew she was trying to control the tempest of her tears.

After a little while they were less violent and when they had almost ceased the Marquis drew a handkerchief from the pocket of his robe and wiped her eyes.

"Would you rather not talk about it to-night?" he asked. "You can sleep and everything you have to tell me can wait until to-morrow."

"No .. I want to .. tell you," she murmured. "And besides I am .. afraid I might .. forget again."

"You will not do that," the Marquis said reassuringly. "But tell me, if you wish to. You know I want to hear everything."

She moved to lie back against the pillows but her hands sought his as if the mere touch of him gave her comfort and support.

"It was .. in the .. boat," she whispered. "We were not far from the .. shore, when the .. man picked up a piece of wood or a .. cudgel, I am not certain which .. and hit .. Grandpapa on the head with it."

She drew in her breath before she could go on:

"He slumped .. forward and his hat fell off .. The man .. hit him .. again and .. again! I suppose I .. screamed. Then .. after he threw .. Grandpapa out of the boat into the .. river he hit me! I remember .. nothing .. more."

Her whole body shook convulsively as she was telling the Marquis what had happened and there was a terror in her eyes he had never thought to see in a woman's face.

"You did not know who the man was?" the Marquis asked quietly.

"No .. he came to the .. farm and told Grandpapa there had been a .. mistake and the person who .. wanted him was on the .. other side of the .. river."

It all sounded a little incoherent and after a moment the Marquis said:

"Start at the beginning, Idylla, if it is not too much

for you. Tell me first of all your name and the name of your Grandfather."

There was a little pause, then Idylla said:

"I use my grandfather's name which is Salford. He was the Vicar of Gore which is a village not far from Goldhanger."

"Goldhanger?" the Marquis exclaimed. "That is the other side of the river."

"Mama and I had lived in the Vicarage with .. Grandpapa ever since I can .. remember," Idylla said, "and when Mama .. died there were only the .. two of us."

"You say that you use your Grandfather's name," the Marquis said. "You do not know your father's name?"

"It sounds .. strange," Idylla replied, "but I have never .. heard his .. name!"

"But you knew him?" the Marquis asked.

"Yes .. but he died when I was eight years old."

"Before that did he live with you at the Vicarage?"

Idylla shook her head.

"No .. but he used to come and see us very often .. yet .."

Her voice ceased as she appeared to hesitate.

"Yet what?" the Marquis prompted.

"I think there was some .. mystery about him," Idylla said. "Mama did not .. explain and when I was a child I could never .. understand why Papa did not live with us as .. other children's fathers .. did."

She paused, then she added:

"I only know that I loved him very much, and when he died I thought Mama's heart would break .. she was so desperately and miserably unhappy."

"But she still did not tell you who he was?"

"Once I asked her," Idylla said, "and she answered: 'All you need to know, Idylla, is that your father was the most wonderful man in the world. We loved each other and we both loved you, my dearest. I used to pray that we could all be together but God has taken him away and we must accept it as God's will.' "

Idylla gave a little sob.

"When she said that Mama cried, and so I thought it best not to talk about Papa any more."

"Now tell me what happened the night your Grandfather was killed," the Marquis said.

"It was quite late in the afternoon," Idylla replied, "when a boy came to the door to say Grandfather was wanted urgently by someone dying on Osea Island."

"There are not many houses on the island," the Marquis remarked.

He knew Osea Island well. It was very small and situated where the river widened.

"I know. There are only two cottages and a farm," Idylla said. "The inhabitants belong to Grandpapa's parish."

"How did you get to the island?" the Marquis asked.

"There was a boat waiting for us at Goldhanger Creek and someone to row us across."

"Why did you go?"

"I forgot to say the boy asked that I should accompany Grandfather so that I could look after the children while he ministered the woman who was dying."

"Did you often do that?" the Marquis asked.

"If it was necessary," Idylla answered. "In the small cottages, if the children were noisy or crying, it was impossible for Grandpapa, who was rather deaf, to hear what the ill person wished to say to him."

"I can understand that," the Marquis said.

"... set out together," Idylla went on, "and as the ... had said it was a case of urgency I just put my thick cloak over the gown I was wearing."

She gave a little sigh.

"I did not think we would be away from home for long."

"Did you tell anyone where you were going?" the Marquis asked.

"There was no-one to tell," Idylla answered. "There is a woman .. Mrs. Laver .. who comes in to clean the Vicarage in the mornings, but I always prepared Grandpapa's evening meal myself."

"So you set out expecting to be back within an hour or so," the Marquis prompted.

"All I took with me was some soup for the sick woman," Idylla said, "and some strawberries which I had picked from the garden for Grandpapa's supper. I thought they might keep the children quiet."

"What happened when you reached the island?" the Marquis asked.

"We went up to the farm which was where I thought the boy had said we were expected," Idylla answered, "but they said they had not sent for us."

"That must have been a surprise," the Marquis remarked.

"It was," Idylla agreed, "but they were pleased to see Grandpapa and asked him to sit down by the fire. One of their sons ran to the cottages to find out who was ill. It was then that .. he came to the .. door!'

Idylla's fingers trembled and the Marquis knew by the expression in her eyes that this was the man who had attempted to kill her.

"What did he look like?" he asked.

"He was dark, with rather a long nose and an

educated voice. I could not see him very well as he did not come in and wore a hat pulled down low over his eye-brows."

"What did he say?" the Marquis asked.

"He said there had been a mistake and the woman who was ill had been taken to the mainland and would Grandpapa come at once?"

"You did not ask him any questions?" the Marquis enquired.

"He seemed to be in such a hurry. I think too, Grandpapa thought we were wasting time if someone was dying. So we hurried away, the man walking quickly ahead of us to where there was a boat."

"A different boat from the one you had been brought to the island in?"

"Yes. It was a slightly bigger one. We got into it and he began to row not as I expected to Goldhanger Creek but across the river!"

"Did you ask him where he was going?"

"I was sitting in the bow and Grandpapa was between me and the man."

She thought the Marquis looked surprised and she explained:

"Grandpapa was very active. He picked up the second pair of oars and sat down in front of me. 'I will give you a hand,' he said to the man, 'it will not take so long.'"

"Your Grandfather said nothing about rowing south instead of north?"

"He might have," Idylla replied. "It seems stupid of me, but I cannot remember. I was worrying that I had left the soup and the strawberries behind at the farm because the man who had come to the door was in such a hurry."

There was a little wrinkle between her eyes as she said:

"Now you mention it I think they must have spoken because I remember thinking that he did not seem to have an Essex accent, and that he spoke like a gentleman."

"Tell me what happened," the Marquis said gently.

"I have told you," Idylla replied. "When I looked over my shoulder I could see in the dim light just before nightfall the outline of the river bank. Then as I turned back again the man was standing up to attack Grandpapa."

The tears came again and now she shut her eyes as they ran down her cheeks.

"It was .. horrible! Ghastly! I could see Grandpapa putting up his .. hands and then being .. thrown into the .. river. I could .. hear the sound his .. body made. The water splashed on my .. cheeks and all over my .. cloak."

The Marquis put his arms around her and held her close again.

"It is all over now," he said, "and I think your Grandfather would be glad that although he died you survived."

"But whoever .. murdered Grandpapa is still .. trying to .. kill me!" Idylla whispered.

The Marquis knew this was irrefutable. There was no other reason why Idylla should have been abducted from the Castle unless the murderer was determined she should not live to tell what happened.

He wondered in fact why the men who had gone to such trouble to abduct her had not just killed her when they entered her bedroom.

Then he thought that despite the ever-mounting number of crimes that were enacted in England every year it was not easy to find men prepared to commit murder when the penalty for doing so was the gallows with no chance of a reprieve.

Thinking it over he was sure that once the men, who were rough, uncouth types, had taken Idylla away from the Castle, the man with the educated voice who had killed her Grandfather would have disposed of her as he had meant to do the first time he hit her.

The whole plan seemed, the Marquis thought, like a puzzle that was beginning to take shape and become a picture that he could see quite clearly.

But he did not wish to upset Idylla any more than she was at the moment by telling her about it.

Although she was still crying against him she was warmer than she had been before and the fire flickering in the grate was casting a golden glow over the room.

"We may be able to find out tomorrow a great deal more than we know now," he said. "But now I want you to try and sleep. If you do not do so, you will not be able to help me, and I need your help."

"How?" she asked.

"I am determined," the Marquis replied, "to bring to justice the man or men who were responsible for your Grandfather's death and who have injured you!"

"I can .. help you?"

Her tears had ceased for the moment and he answered:

"It is essential you should do so and that is why I want you to make a real effort to sleep through what is left of the night. But because I think you might be afraid alone, I will stay here with you and sleep on the sofa."

"You will be .. uncomfortable," Idylla said.

"I have slept in far worse places," the Marquis answered. "Someday I will tell you about them, but only if you will go to sleep now."

He thought she looked worried and added:

"If you prefer, I could awaken Nanny. But I feel there would be so many explanations to make to her and a lot of questions to answer. It will be far better if you will allow me to do things my way."

"I .. would much .. rather you .. stayed with me."

"I hoped you would say that," the Marquis answered.

He rose from the bed and pulled the bed-clothes up under her chin.

"Shut your eyes and try to go to sleep," he said, "otherwise you will feel ill and be useless to me to-morrow."

"I .. want to .. help you," Idylla murmured.

She turned over like a child and put her cheek against the pillow.

The Marquis tucked in the blankets and resisting an impulse to kiss her cheek blew out the lights in the candelabra.

He lay down on the comfortable satin sofa which stood on one side of the fireplace.

He told himself as he did so that he would wake at six o'clock so that he would have left Idylla's room long before there was any chance of Nanny coming in to see how her patient was.

When he was in the Army the Marquis had trained himself to wake up at any time he wished. And he knew as he closed his eyes and relaxed his body that he would be awake at exactly six o'clock.

There was a great deal he wanted to think about but he deliberately stopped his mind working, because he was determined to be at his most alert and intelligent the following day.

The mystery over Idylla was gradually unravelling itself, but there was still a great deal more to discover.

The Marquis was determined, as he had never been determined about anything in his life, that he would bring to the gallows the man who had tried to destroy anything so exquisite, if it was the last thing he ever did.

.   .   .   .   .

When the Marquis looked at the two men who had tried to abduct Idylla the night before he found them sorry-looking creatures.

There was blood which had dripped onto their faces from the blows he had inflicted on their heads, and having passed the night trussed up by the night-watchmen, they were stiff, and looked with their unshaven dirty faces extremely unprepossessing.

He found, as he had expected, that they had little of importance to tell him.

They had come from the slums of Shoreditch. There they had met a gentleman in an Inn who had promised them £10 each if they would steal away a young woman on whom he had set his fancy.

The gentleman had told them exactly what they were to do, and had provided them with a cart and a horse in which they were to drive Idylla, gagged and bound, to the Lowring Creek.

The cart and the horse had been found where they had left them tied to a tree in the park, and although he questioned and cross-questioned the two men, and later they were interrogated by the High Sheriff himself, the Marquis was certain they could tell him little more than they had done already.

The High Sheriff ordered them to be conveyed to Chelmsford where they would be put in prison awaiting trial.

Then the Marquis took Colonel Trumble into the Library and told him the whole story leading up to the moment when he had seen Idylla being let down from the balcony of her bedroom into the garden.

"It was a clever idea, My Lord!" the Colonel said, "and it was certainly not thought out by those scally-wags with whom we have been talking."

"There is a master-mind behind this," the Marquis said. "A man activated not only by hatred but also, I am convinced, by greed!"

"What makes you think that, My Lord?" the Colonel asked.

"What I am going to tell you is of course confidential," the Marquis replied, "and for the moment based merely on supposition. I have no proof and it is going to be difficult to find it; but I am absolutely convinced that when I do, this fiend who has disposed of the Vicar of Gorc, and very nearly his granddaughter also, will receive the sentence of death he so rightly deserves!"

"Tell me exactly what it is you suspect," the Colonel asked.

The Marquis told him.

.   .   .   .   .

They talked together for over an hour and when the High Sheriff left the Castle the Marquis walked with him to the front door.

"It is pleasant to meet you, My Lord," Colonel Trumble said, "and I am delighted that you are staying here. I have always admired the Castle and have longed for the day when it would be opened and I should know that its owner was in residence."

"I see I have been very remiss in not coming to Essex more often," the Marquis replied. "I suppose in a way it was because I was so happy here as a boy, I was afraid that if I returned, I might be disappointed."

"And have you been?" the Colonel enquired.

"On the contrary, I have found it more enjoyable than ever before!" the Marquis replied.

"Then I hope you will stay a long time and come again," the High Sheriff said. "I expect Roger Clarke has already told you we have had a good nesting season?"

The Marquis smiled.

"I have already informed Clarke that he may expect me in September, and I hope, Colonel, that you will join me in several shoots."

"I should be delighted to accept any invitation Your Lordship may extend to me," the High Sheriff said with sincerity.

As he drove away in his smart carriage which bore the Sheriff's arms on the door, Colonel Trumble was smiling.

The Marquis went upstairs to Idylla's bedroom.

She was dressed and sitting outside on the balcony, and he knew by the expression on her face that she had been waiting anxiously for his appearance.

"What has happened?" she asked. "I thought you would never come and tell me!"

"There is unfortunately very little to tell," the Marquis answered.

He thought as he sat down beside her that despite the terror of the night before she looked amazingly beautiful and not unduly perturbed.

Then his eyes met hers and he understood.

He could not be mistaken in recognising when a woman was happy because he was with her. The light in Idylla's eyes, the soft curve of her lips and the faint flush on her pale cheeks told him without words exactly what she was feeling.

"Before we talk about anything else," he said, "I want to know how well you slept, and how you feel this morning."

He glanced over his shoulder to see that Nanny was not in the bedroom and could not overhear.

"When I left you very early this morning you were sleeping peacefully and, I hope, dreaming of me."

The colour which rose in her face was very beautiful.

"I think I was .. dreaming of you," she answered, "because when I awoke I was no longer .. frightened, but happy .. very happy!"

"And you are happy now?" he asked.

"Now that you are here," she answered. "It just seemed a long time while I was waiting."

"It seemed a long time to me too," the Marquis answered truthfully, "but I had to give you time to get dressed, and I also had to talk to the High Sheriff."

"You told him about Grandpapa?"

"He already knew. It had been reported to him officially that the Vicar of Gore and his granddaughter were missing, but he had not taken the information seriously. He explained to me that a great number of people go on holidays or are called away to

152

dying relatives without informing anyone of their destination."

"Of course," Idylla murmured.

"Now he will send one of his officials to the Vicarage," the Marquis said. "They will inform your Grandfather's parishioners of what has happened and ensure that the house is locked so that nothing can be stolen."

"I do not think anyone from the village would steal from us," Idylla said.

Then after a moment in a different tone she asked:

"They have not . . found . . Grandpapa's body?"

"Not yet, but the High Sheriff is going to make enquiries. As you know, the tide might have taken his body out to sea, in which case it might be cast up on another shore."

"I . . understand," Idylla said.

"There is one thing I wanted to ask you," the Marquis said. "Where did your Grandfather keep the Church Register? The one in which is written all the births, deaths and marriages?"

"In the Vestry," Idylla answered. "You will find it in a drawer at the bottom of a wardrobe where Grandpapa hung his surplice."

"Thank you. That is what I wanted to know," the Marquis replied.

"Why are you interested?" she asked.

"That is something I hope to explain to you later," the Marquis answered. "For the moment, I want you – and it is very important, Idylla, – to try to get well as quickly as possible."

"But I am well," Idylla said. "Nanny said that if it had not been for what happened last night she was going to suggest that I went for a walk in the garden."

She looked into the Marquis's eyes and added :

"I did so want you to show me the flowers and where you played when you were a little boy."

"We will do that to-morrow," the Marquis promised. "But get well quickly because I have some other important plans for us both."

"Something we can do together?" Idylla asked eagerly.

"Together!" he answered.

He bent forward as he spoke and took her hand in his.

"It is too soon and I meant to wait," he said. "But after what happened last night I am so afraid of losing you, of your disappearing when I am not actually touching you and holding you in my arms."

He felt a little quiver run through her. Then he said :

"Will you marry me, Idylla?"

He saw her eyes widen. He knew that this was something she had not expected him to say even though he was sure that she loved him.

As if the full significance of what he had asked swept over her like a wave in the sea, there was a dazzling light in her eyes and a radiance in her face which made her look even more beautiful than before.

"It is very .. wonderful of you to ask me to be your wife .. but you know I cannot .. accept."

"Why not?" the Marquis enquired. "I love you, Idylla, and let me tell you that I have never before asked any woman to be my wife! I have never loved anyone, my darling, as I love you!"

She did not answer and after a moment he said :

"When I ran downstairs last night to prevent those men from carrying you away, I knew that if I lost you

I would have lost everything that really mattered to me in life."

A faint smile touched his lips as he went on :

"I would have lost 'perfection' something which I have sought always, only to be disappointed. How could I have guessed, or even imagined, I should find it in rescuing a witch from being ducked in the village pond ?"

There was a little silence, then Idylla said hesitatingly :

"It is . . because you have sought . . perfection and because everything you do is . . perfect, that I cannot . . marry you."

"I do not understand," the Marquis said.

"I have remembered my name and I know now I am not a witch," Idylla said, "but I do not know the name of my . . father. I cannot . . now that I think about it, even be . . sure that he and Mama were . . married to each other !"

She bent her head as she spoke and the Marquis knew it was to hide the colour which now rose almost painfully from her small chin up to her forehead.

"How could you," she asked in a voice barely above a whisper, "who are so important . . so distinguished . . marry a . . love-child ?"

There was a tenderness in the Marquis's eyes that had never been there before.

"If you are thinking for me, Idylla," he said, "which I know you are, let me assure you that however you may have been born, whoever your parents may be, I should feel honoured and fortunate above all men if you consented to be my wife. But I want to tell you something."

Idylla's head was still bent and after a moment he said :

"Look at me, my darling, and listen to what I have to say."

Obediently she raised her head and her blue eyes looked into his.

"I am convinced in my own mind," he said, "that not only were your father and mother married, but that he was in fact of distinguished birth of whom you can well be proud. But this is something that has to be proved, and that is why I am asking you, my beloved, to trust me — just trust me a little longer, until there is no more mystery to trouble and upset you."

Idylla drew in her breath and once again the light was back in her eyes.

"I love you!" she said. "You know I love you! But I would not do anything to .. harm you, and I know that because you are who you are .. to marry me as things are at the moment would be wrong .. very wrong! You might .. regret it."

"I would never regret marrying you," the Marquis said. "You are all I have dreamt of or imagined might exist somewhere in the world, if only I could find it. But I do understand what you are trying to say to me."

He looked at her searchingly as if he would impress her loveliness on his mind. Then he said :

"I cannot believe that anyone can be so perfect in every way, and that is why I will never rest, Idylla, until you belong to me completely and absolutely!"

"That is what I want," she whispered, "but I am thinking for .. you."

"In a way no-one has ever thought for me before," the Marquis answered.

He knew as he spoke that no woman could be more unselfish, more high-principled, than to deny her heart simply because she thought it might harm him socially.

"We are going to be married!" he said masterfully. "You are going to belong to me, my lovely one, and all the terrible things that have happened to you will be forgotten."

"But at the moment," Idylla said in a very small voice, "the man who .. killed Grandpapa is still waiting to .. kill me!"

She gave an exclamation that was like a cry.

"In doing so he might harm you," she said. "You must promise me to be careful .. very careful! Supposing .."

She gave a little gasp of fear.

"Supposing, because you prevented me from being .. drowned as a witch and being .. abducted last night, he now tries to take his .. vengeance on .. you?"

"So you are afraid for me rather than for yourself!" the Marquis said in a voice that had an incredulous note in it. "Oh, my sweet, could anyone be so entrancing, so angelic in every way?"

He lifted her hands to his lips and kissed them passionately one after the other. Then as he felt a tremor run through her and knew he excited her, his lips found hers.

It was a kiss as perfect and even more ecstatic in a different way than the one they had exchanged the night before.

Now the Marquis's lips were more possessive, more demanding, and as he felt Idylla respond to his need of her there was a glint of fire in his eyes.

"I love you! God, how I love you!" he said. "Let us be married at once, my precious. Why should we wait?"

"Please .. please .. do not tempt me," Idylla pleaded. "I know I must do what is right for .. you. You cannot marry me until I know who my father .. was."

She hid her face against his shoulder. Then she said in a very small, child-like voice :

"S . suppose .. we never .. find out ?"

"Then I must either wait for you until we are old and grey and too decrepit to walk up the aisle," the Marquis said with a touch of laughter in his voice, "or I shall have to carry you away by sheer force and make you my wife whether you consent or not !"

She gave a little choked laugh, but when she raised her head she said seriously :

"Please .. please do not make it more .. difficult for me than it is already to say .. 'no' to you. I did not know a man could be so .. magnificent .. and yet so .. considerate and gentle."

"I shall never be anything else to you," the Marquis said, and she knew it was a vow as sacred as if he made it in front of the altar.

.   .   .   .   .   .

Later that evening Roger Clarke came into the Library where the Marquis was waiting for him, carrying a large leather-bound book in his arms.

"You have found it !" the Marquis exclaimed rising from the desk where he had been writing.

"I have found it, My Lord, exactly where you said it would be," Roger Clarke replied.

He set the book down on the desk and went on :

"The High Sheriff's men were waiting when I arrived. I did not think you would wish to tell Miss

Idylla, My Lord, but the Vicarage has been ransacked from the basement to the attic!"

"Ransacked?" the Marquis exclaimed. "But why, and by whom?"

"The Villagers were protesting that they had nothing to do with it and did not even know it had occurred. The woman who works there, a Mrs Laver, said it had been done at night. She had locked up the house after she found the Vicar and Miss Idylla had vanished, but someone had got in by breaking one of the windows. It was quite obvious, My Lord, there had been a systematic search."

"Had anything been taken?" the Marquis asked.

"Mrs. Laver thought not. The silver was there and a few trinkets belonging to Miss Idylla. The china and pictures were not disturbed, but every drawer in the place had been thrown to the floor, every cupboard opened, and every book pulled from the bookcases!"

"Then I have a feeling," the Marquis said slowly, "that what I am looking for in this Register will not be there."

He opened the leather-bound book as he spoke.

The records went back over fifty years and he turned over the pages impatiently until he came to the years after 1780.

Then he went very slowly until near 1781 and 1782 both the pages were missing.

They had obviously been torn out carefully but there were still tiny pieces of the stiff paper in the binding to mark the place where they had been.

"I am afraid, My Lord, it was a wasted journey," Roger Clarke said.

"Not wasted," the Marquis said, "it only confirms what I expected to have happened."

The young man waited as if hoping that the Marquis would enlighten him further, but he merely closed the Register and said:

"I should be grateful, Clarke, if you would take this back at your convenience, but I should put it in a place of safety. The village will not wish to lose a record of such importance to those who feature in it."

"Is there anything I can do in the Vicarage itself, My Lord?"

"I do not think so," the Marquis answered. "I imagine Mrs. Laver, or whatever her name is, will gradually tidy it up and as you have already guessed, I shall not speak about it to Miss Idylla. It would only upset her and there is no point in her knowing what has happened."

"I suppose not – until she returns," Roger Clarke said.

"If she returns," the Marquis murmured enigmatically.

.   .   .   .   .

The Marquis had luncheon with Idylla on the balcony in the sunshine.

He made her laugh and they talked of many things, but not of the problem which occupied both their minds almost to the exclusion of all else.

The Marquis decided that the less said in front of the servants about last night the better.

He knew that Nanny and through her the whole household thought the attempt to kidnap Idylla had been by someone local who was still convinced she was a witch.

"The ignorant heathens in this part of the world," Nanny said scornfully, "are so afraid of magic that they themselves become demons in trying to stamp it out."

"Whatever the reason for such behaviour," the Marquis said quietly, "it is something that will not occur again at the Castle. I have already arranged with Mr. Clarke that there will be two men patrolling the grounds with dogs every night. Everyone can therefore sleep peacefully in their beds, unless of course the dogs keep them awake by barking."

He smiled as he spoke but Nanny said seriously:

"I'll not have have them witch-hunters nor anyone else making Miss Idylla ill again. I've got her well, and well she'll stay, or I'll know the reason why!"

"That is right, Nanny," the Marquis approved, "and I shall want to know the reason why too, so the less everyone talks about it the better!"

He soon learnt that any fears the servants had entertained regarding Idylla had been swept away by this new development.

They were outraged that outsiders had actually entered the Castle, and to all intents and purposes had tried to steal from it.

"It's an impertinence, M'Lord!" Newman said. "It has made the footmen so angry that I think they would have battered those men unmercifully if the Sheriff's men had not taken them away."

"I am grateful for their feelings of loyalty," the Marquis said.

"I thought you would wish to know, M'Lord, that the two men who left us when Miss Idylla first arrived have asked to be re-instated."

The Marquis smiled.

"I hope you will be merciful and forgive them for being so nervous, Newman."

"I do not intend to be too magnanimous over-quickly, M'Lord. It'll do no harm for them to cool their heels a bit. They'll not find another job like this easily in these parts!"

"Not with Sir Caspar sacking his staff!" the Marquis remarked.

He decided when luncheon was over and Nanny insisted Idylla should rest that he would make another attempt to see Caspar Trydell.

He had a great deal to say to him and some very pertinent questions to ask him.

But when he arrived at Trydell Hall it was to be told by Bates that Sir Caspar had left for London first thing in the morning.

"He was here yesterday, M'Lord," Bates said, "and as I knew you wished to see him I very nearly sent a message up to the Castle. But I was sure Sir Caspar would stay a day or two; in fact I think that was his original intention."

"What changed his mind?" the Marquis asked.

"I don't know, M'Lord, and that's a fact! This morning he came down in a bad mood. Cross as two sticks he was — as we used to say when we were young — and finding fault with everything and everybody. He orders his curricle and drives back to London."

"You do not expect him back again?" the Marquis asked.

"No, M'Lord."

The Marquis hesitated, then he enquired:

"Did he take anything with him?"

He glanced at a space on the wall as he spoke and knew that Bates understood.

"The last picture in the Drawing-Room, M'Lord. It was Her Ladyship's favourite, although actually Mr. Chiswick told me it had no great value."

"Sir Caspar has sold a great deal, I believe?" the Marquis ventured.

"See for yourself, M'Lord," Bates answered.

He walked across the hall and opened the door of the Dining-Room.

Here the Marquis remembered had hung some very fine examples of Stubbs's horses, of Herring's racing pictures, and one or two portraits of previous Trydells of which John had always been extremely proud.

One, of a General Trydell who had served under Marlborough, might have been John himself, and the Marquis felt with a surge of annoyance that a man must have sunk very low when he sold his ancestors off the walls.

"Why should Sir Caspar be so hard-up?" he enquired

"Gaming, M'Lord! He's always been the same! Sir Caspar once told me that his fingers itched for cards, and that, I believe, is the right expression."

"It is indeed," the Marquis answered.

He walked from the room because he found it distressing to see the marks on the walls where the pictures had hung, and to think of Caspar Trydell throwing away a long history of decent and distinguished ancestors simply because his fingers 'itched' when he sat at a green-baize table.

The Marquis rode back to the Castle pensively.

It was getting late and he went straight to his bedroom to bathe and change for dinner.

He had already arranged for Idylla to dine with him and when he entered the Sitting-Room where they had dined the night before she was not lying on the *chaise longue* but standing at the window with her back to him.

The Marquis shut the door and as if without words he called her home, she turned swiftly and gave a little cry of sheer joy!

Then she ran across the room as eagerly as a child to throw herself into his arms.

"My darling! My sweet!" he exclaimed. "I have missed you!"

"It seems .. a century since .. luncheon-time," she whispered.

"That is what I felt too," the Marquis answered.

Then he was kissing her passionately, frantically, as if he was afraid of losing her.

7

The Marquis stood looking out into the garden.

The rhododendrons were a crimson splash of colour against the purple and white of the lilacs, and bushes of syringa, delicate and ethereal scented the air.

The sun was sinking but it was still a blaze of glory and the Marquis wondered if anything could be more beautiful.

He thought that he had been happier these last weeks at the Castle than he had ever been before, and he knew it was due to Idylla.

Never in his whole life had he known such ecstasy combined with a contentment which was inexpressible.

If he obeyed his impulse, he thought, he would stay here forever and never go back to the social world which made so many different demands upon him.

Here he and Idylla lived as if they were in an enchanted Castle and the wildness of Essex were an uncharted sea.

Then with a sigh which seemed to come from the very depths of his being the Marquis lifted to his eyes the letter he held in his hand.

It was from George Summers.

A groom who had fetched some things the Marquis required from London had called at Aldridge House and been given it by Mr. Graham.

George Summers wrote as he talked, fluently and amusingly and the Marquis read :

"*Heaven knows where you have hidden yourself Oswin. The social world is in a twitter at your disappearance. The Prince is outraged that you should find any place on earth more attractive than Carlton House. But I must inform you that great events have taken place since you were here!*

As you will remember Mrs. Fitzherbert sent an emissary from the Roman Catholic Church in Warwick Street to lay her case before the Pope.

It was frankly to ask whether she could be right to return to the Prince after he has married Princess Caroline.

As you know, before you left the Prince's frantic desire that Mrs. Fitz. would take him back had become such a frenzy that we feared he might be near to losing his reason.

The day after you left London he became so ill that he could not hold a pen in his hand and he is completely convinced that if he had not 'been bereft of sense' he would have killed himself!

We none of us knew what to do for the best; but now, thank goodness, the Papal decision has been made known. Mrs. Fitz. may rejoin the Prince, 'who is her lawful husband in the eyes of the Church.'

Needless to say a great number of Statesmen are disgusted and even apprehensive about the decision while H.R.H.'s friends are overjoyed. He and Mrs. Fitz. are once more inseparable.

Mrs. Fitz. has decided to give a public breakfast for the Prince as a way of announcing to society that a formal reunion has taken place.

I am told on good authority that no fewer than 400 guests have been invited, and despite the fact that some of the more stiff-necked hostesses are shocked at what is happening, you can wager your last penny that they will all be there.

Quite frankly, I think you should be present. You have always been a close friend of H.R.H. and I am certain he will take it extremely ill if your only excuse is that you prefer the country."

George Summers finished his letter with some references to several parties he had enjoyed of a less reputable nature and gave the Marquis the results of a Mill in which they had both bet on the victor.

The Marquis was however concerned with the information about Mrs. Fitzherbert's party.

He knew that not only would it annoy the Prince and perhaps hurt him if he did not make an appearance, but it would also cause a considerable amount of comment.

What was more, he had an idea that to attend the function might ultimately prove to his advantage.

While he was thinking about it, the door opened and Idylla walked into the room.

She was looking exceedingly beautiful in a gown of soft green which made the Marquis think of the sea.

Her eyes were very blue as she moved towards him with a smile on her lips, and he saw that Nanny for the first time, had allowed her to dress her hair high on her head.

The Marquis raised both her hands to his lips and when he had kissed them one after the other he said:

"I am glad to see you are finally and completely no longer an invalid."

"I am well," Idylla said and her voice was like a

paean of happiness. "Even Nanny can no longer pretend that the wound on my head has not healed or that I am anything but robustly healthy!"

"That is hardly the adverb I would have used," the Marquis said, "but I am glad you are well, my darling."

"May I come riding with you to-morrow?"

"I have other plans to tell you about," the Marquis said, "but first let us have dinner."

They dined in the great Dining-Hall, decorated with murals, which was one of the finest rooms in the Castle.

But Idylla had eyes only for the Marquis even while they talked on many different subjects. She loved learning from him and hearing him explain so much she had always wanted to know.

But she felt all the time their hearts talked to each other in a secret manner which only they could understand.

When dinner was over they walked back to the Salon, and now the sun was a glow of crimson and gold low in the west. The shadows in the garden were purple and mysterious and the fragrance which came through the windows was from the night-scented stocks.

Idylla seated herself on the sofa. Then as the Marquis sat down in a high wing-back armchair opposite her she said:

"There is something .. troubling you."

He smiled because they were so closely attuned to each other that it was impossible for either of them not to know what the other was thinking.

"I am not really troubled, my darling," he said. "It is just that I am a little apprehensive about what I have to say to you."

"What is it?" Idylla asked.

"I want you to come to London with me."

"To .. London?"

He heard the surprise in her voice and saw a little flicker of nervousness in her eyes.

"But why must we leave .. here where we are so .. happy," she asked.

"One reason," the Marquis replied, "is that although like you I am happier here than I have ever been before, you will still not consent to marry me and I have to find the evidence that will convince you that it is imperative for you to become my wife."

"And you think you will find .. that in .. London?"

"I think so," the Marquis said with a note of sincerity in his voice. "I have tried to find here what we seek and while I am convinced in my own mind that I have the answer to every question where you are concerned, there is still something missing — still something which once I have it in my hands will convince you."

Idylla did not answer and the Marquis said:

"I love you, my darling! I cannot go on indefinitely without knowing you are safe because you will always be beside me not only in the day-time but also at night."

He paused, then he said:

"I wake a dozen times after I have gone to bed afraid, despite all the precautions I have taken, that something might harm you."

There was a note in his voice which told Idylla that his fears were very real to him.

She rose from the sofa to kneel down beside him and turned her face up to his.

"I love you!" she said softly. "I would not have you think that I do not wish to do what you ask of me. I want more than anything .. more than my hope of Heaven .. to be your .. wife."

Her eyes dropped and the colour rose in her cheeks as she said in a low voice he could hardly hear:

"I too am sometimes .. afraid at night, and then I .. pretend I am .. close to you and in your .. arms."

"And that is where you should be!" the Marquis said. "Marry me before we go to London, Idylla! Then I will know that you trust me and believe that I will find the solution to everything sooner or later."

She raised her head to look up at him as she said:

"I was thinking last night how much you have given me and how little I have given you in return. Then I thought that I love you not only because we belong to each other as a .. man and a woman .. but also as your mother would have loved you .. had she lived."

The Marquis put his fingers gently against her cheek as Idylla continued:

"Nanny told me how lonely you were when you came here as a boy, how your father did not want you and there was no-one to love you as you should have been loved."

Idylla's voice was very moving as she went on:

"That is the love I want to give you .. I want to make up to you for all you have .. missed."

She paused, then she said very softly:

"That is why I cannot risk hurting you in any way, as I might do if you married me not knowing who I am."

"I know who you are," the Marquis said. "I am sure of it, but I cannot as yet prove it."

He saw the question in Idylla's eyes and he went on:

"That, my precious one, is why I will tell you what

I suspect and believe only when the proof is there and the whole world will know the truth."

"We will wait," Idylla whispered, "but I will pray with all my heart and all my soul that it will not be .. long."

"As I am praying already," the Marquis answered.

.   .   .   .   .

In the gardens at Castle House, Ealing, three marquees had been erected for the accommodation of the company who had been invited to meet at two o'clock, while the dinner was to be at seven.

There were bands playing continuously.

The flowers that grew by nature in the garden had been augmented by fantastic arrangements from the florists, which were already wilting slightly in the heat despite, the Marquis knew, the amount that had been expended on them.

Everyone who could ever claim acquaintanceship with the Prince of Wales was present, and all those who had cold-shouldered Mrs. Fitzherbert after the separation between her and His Royal Highness were now endeavouring to ingratiate themselves with her once again.

The Marquis however had always remained on excellent terms with Mrs. Fitzherbert because he considered her a far better and more restraining influence on the Prince than any other woman on whom he had bestowed his favour.

When the Marquis appeared with Idylla Mrs. Fitzherbert held out both her hands with a cry of welcome.

"I did so hope we should see you here this afternoon,

My Lord. The Prince has been extremely distressed by your long absence."

"I am back now," the Marquis answered, "and it was very kind of you to allow me to bring Miss Salford with me."

Mrs. Fitzherbert smiled at Idylla as she curtsied and went on eagerly to the Marquis :

"There is so much to tell you. We shall be extremely poor, but as merry as crickets ! "

"That is all that matters," the Marquis said.

Then as other guests were announced he gave his arm to Idylla and they moved through the marquee, the Marquis being greeted by innumerable friends, none of whom made any effort to disguise their curiosity concerning his companion.

Idylla was looking exceedingly lovely in a gown that had been waiting for her at Aldridge House when they arrived.

The Marquis's unerring taste combined with Madame Valerie's had evolved a gown that while fashionable had an individuality about it which made it as unique as Idylla was herself.

She wore no jewellery except for the diamond cross, but the Marquis knew she had an aura about her which made her glitter even in the company of bejewelled and decorated beauties.

When they had arrived at Aldridge House from Essex, an elderly cousin of the Marquis, who lived in Islington, was waiting for them in the Library which overlooked the garden at the back of the house.

The Marquis had sent a groom post-haste from the Castle to ask her to be his guest and to chaperon a young lady whom he was bringing with him to London.

Lady Constance Howard, who had found life extremely dreary since the death of her husband, was only too willing to oblige her illustrious relative.

She had been invited to Aldridge House only once or twice before and she could hardly believe her good fortune that the Marquis should require her services and that she would have the privilege of staying there.

She was a genuine person with a kind, uncomplicated nature which the Marquis knew would not frighten Idylla, and he was sure she would like her.

He had not been mistaken.

The two women took to each other on sight and Lady Constance told the Marquis confidentially that Idylla was the most attractive and charming young girl she had ever met.

"Wherever did you find anyone so unusual, Oswin?" she enquired.

The Marquis knew she was consumed with curiosity, but he did not for the moment wish to offer any explanation which undoubtedly would be repeated around the family.

"I will tell you all about it later on," he said, "and thank you, Cousin Constance, for coming to my rescue when I needed a Chaperon."

"There is no need to thank me," Lady Constance replied. "It is very exciting to be here and you know I am always prepared to do anything you want me to do."

She smiled, then added:

"As indeed must be most women of your acquaintance!"

The Marquis was careful to introduce Idylla to all his special friends in the social world.

He was well aware that to overlook anyone would be

to create a quite unnecessary hostility not only against himself but also against Idylla.

Fortunately the Marquis had learnt when he returned to London that Lady Brampton was in the country with her husband who was seriously ill.

The Duchess of Devonshire was charming, as she always was, and even the Countess of Harrowly praised Idylla to her face and asked the Marquis where he could have discovered such a masterpiece.

The Marquis's men friends were even more fulsome in their compliments, and the Prince of Wales when he had recovered from being slightly petulant about the Marquis's long absence, with his connoisseur's eye, recognised Idylla's beauty and had a great deal to say about it.

They had in fact just been talking to the Prince and were moving into the garden because the marquees had become so uncomfortably warm, when at the opening of the tent they almost bumped into a man who was just entering it.

Idylla was holding the Marquis's arm and he felt her start, then cling to him almost convulsively, and saw the reason for it.

Caspar Trydell was standing just in front of them.

If Idylla was perturbed at seeing him he was certainly taken aback at seeing her.

For a moment he was rigid and his face seemed almost contorted with surprise and another emotion to which the Marquis did not wish to put a name.

Then, with what was obviously a superhuman effort at self-control, he looked straight at the Marquis and said:

"I am surprised to see you here, Aldridge. I understood you had taken up residence indefinitely in Essex."

"I found it difficult not to be present on such an auspicious occasion," the Marquis replied.

"Of course," Sir Caspar said, "but doubtless Essex will miss you."

His words were casual enough in themselves, but he spoke with an undercurrent of enmity that was very obvious and seemed to hang on the air between the two men. Then Sir Caspar bowed and without looking again at Idylla walked away.

The Marquis knew she was trembling and he drew her outside into the garden.

"That .. man!" she said in a strangled voice. "He .. killed Grandpapa!"

"That is what I suspected," the Marquis said, "but I wanted you to identify him."

He was speaking calmly and soothingly and he drew Idylla away from the crowds to a quiet part of the garden where they could sit down on a seat.

"I could .. not be .. mistaken," she faltered, "and I think he .. recognised me!"

"I know he did!" the Marquis agreed. "And I felt sure that when you saw Caspar Trydell you would know he was the man who took you and your Grandfather out in the boat."

Idylla did not speak and he went on as if giving her time to compose herself :

"I had the feeling that having come to London he would not return to the country. His servant, Bates, told me that he had sent orders for the house to be closed."

"Because he wished to avoid me?" Idylla asked.

"He was sure you would recognise him," the Marquis said, "and that is why he tried to abduct you."

"What .. will he .. do now?" Idylla asked in a very small voice.

"I will tell you what I intend to do a little later," the Marquis answered. "For the moment I want you to forget Caspar Trydell and enjoy yourself."

Because Idylla thought that by making a fuss she would spoil the party for the Marquis and his pleasure in seeing his friends, she controlled her fear and her anxiety in a manner which he thought was quite exceptional.

She was very pale, but she managed to talk intelligently with the gentleman who sat on her other side at dinner. He declared to all and sundry that she was 'entrancing' and would be acclaimed an 'Incomparable' by the Bucks of St. James's before the week was out.

Finally the enormous dinner with the innumerable courses which the Prince enjoyed came to an end, and the guests moved into the garden in search of fresh air.

There was to be dancing and a special floor had been laid under the trees which sparkled with fairy-lights, as did the flower-beds and the edges of the paths which led to arbours discreetly arranged in the shrubbery.

"I think this is where we can escape without being noticed," the Marquis said quietly.

"Will the party go on for a long time?" Idylla enquired.

"I should be very surprised if it concludes before five o'clock tomorrow morning," the Marquis replied.

She looked at him in astonishment but without making any farewells to their hostess he took her round to the front of the house where the carriages were waiting.

It was still comparatively early and as they drove back

to Berkeley Square Idylla said, slipping her hand into the Marquis's :

"I would have liked to dance with you."

"We will do that another night," he answered, lifting her hand to his lips so that he could kiss each finger, one after the other.

"Perhaps I will not . . dance well . . enough," Idylla said a little hesitatingly, "but Mama taught me and she was a very good dancer when she was young."

"I am sure you will find that our steps match perfectly," the Marquis assured her, "as we match each other in everything else, my precious one."

When they entered Aldridge House the Butler said :

"Lady Constance asked me to inform Your Lordship that she has retired for the night. I do not think she expected Your Lordship back so early."

The Marquis acknowledged the information with a nod of his head and drew Idylla into the Library.

The windows were open into the garden which looked very quiet and peaceful in the moonlight after the twinkling lights and noise of Mrs. Fitzherbert's.

The Marquis put his arm round Idylla's shoulders and drew her to the window.

After a moment he said :

"Do you trust me, my precious ?"

Idylla looked up at him in surprise.

"You know I do !" she answered. "I trust you and I love you !"

"And I love you !" the Marquis replied. "I did not know that any woman could be so sweet, so adorable and so utterly and completely desirable !"

His voice deepened on the last word and there was a flicker of fire in his eyes as he looked down at her.

"What are you .. trying to say to .. me?" Idylla asked.

With her usual perception where he was concerned she knew there was something on his mind.

"I want you to do exactly what I tell you to do," the Marquis said.

"But you know I will do that," Idylla replied.

"It may seem a little strange," the Marquis went on, "and it may even seem dangerous; but I promise you, my sweetheart, it will not be dangerous, and I shall protect you even if I am not actually standing beside you."

Idylla looked up at him in bewilderment.

"What are you saying to me?" she asked. "What are you trying to tell me?"

The Marquis paused a moment before he said:

"I want you, darling, to walk into the garden alone. I want you to walk casually onto the lawn and stand there turning your head up towards the stars just as you might do when you are thinking of our love and from where it comes."

Idylla looked at him in perplexity.

"You want me to do .. this .. now?"

"I want you to do it exactly five minutes after you have heard me leave the house," the Marquis said with a note of authority in his voice.

"Leave the house?" Idylla exclaimed. "But where are you going?"

"I have told you to trust me," he answered. "To believe that I will not leave you and that you are safe – completely safe, however it may appear to the contrary."

He ceased speaking and putting his fingers under her chin raised her face to his.

"There is only one thing to remember and one thing only," he said, "and that is that I love you with all my heart and all my soul. You are mine, Idylla, and I will never lose you!"

His lips sought hers and he felt a quiver of excitement run through her because she was in his arms.

It was a long kiss and a passionate one.

When finally he released her her lips were parted and he knew that her heart was beating tumultuously and her eyes were soft with the feelings he evoked in her.

"I love you! I love you!" she whispered. "I did not know it was possible to feel like this and still be upon earth!"

"Then go and look at the stars, my precious one," the Marquis said, "and imagine that I am carrying you to the moon and we are leaving behind everything that is wicked and evil."

He turned away from the window as he spoke and looked towards the clock on the mantelshelf.

"Wait exactly five minutes after you have heard the carriage drive away. I will leave the door open so that you cannot be mistaken."

Idylla looked at him with a puzzled expression in her eyes. But he knew because she loved him so completely that she would do as he wished, and would never argue or plague him with questions as another woman might have done.

'It is the little things as well as the big ones that makes real love so different from the false,' the Marquis thought to himself.

He walked across the Hall, took his hat from the Butler and stepped into the carriage which was waiting for him outside.

Idylla heard the front door close and looked at the clock.

It was almost exactly half past eleven.

She walked across the Salon to close the door. Then she stood looking around the candlelit room and thought as she had done ever since coming to Aldridge House what a perfect background it was for the Marquis.

It was impossible to imagine how the decorations could be improved or what better pictures could replace those that hung on the walls, or the treasures that were arranged in every Salon.

"Everything about him is so magnificent, and at the same time he is so human and understanding, kind and gentle," Idylla told herself.

She had no idea that a great number of people would have been greatly surprised at hearing the Marquis described in such terms.

"I love him! I love him!" she whispered and watched the clock until it was exactly five and twenty minutes to the hour.

Then slowly and casually she walked through the open window and down the three steps which led into the garden.

It was very quiet for London she thought, and the trees silhouetted against the starlit sky gave her the impression of being in the country.

There was the fragrance of flowers and she half-expected to hear a nightingale sing.

She moved across the grass that felt like velvet beneath her satin slippers.

When she reached the centre of the small lawn she turned her face up to the stars as the Marquis had told her to do and imagined he was carrying her towards the sky and his lips were on hers.

Her imagination was so vivid that a man advancing from the shadows had almost reached her before she realised he was there and she dropped her eyes to look at him.

She gave a start of sheer horror and her hands went up to her breasts.

It was Caspar Trydell! She could see the evil in his face combined with the murderous hatred that she had last seen when he struck her Grandfather on the head and bludgeoned him to death.

"You!"

She was not certain whether she said the words aloud. She only knew that the mere sight of him made it impossible to move, impossible to breathe.

"Yes, it is I!" Caspar Trydell answered in a low voice that sounded like the hiss of a reptile. "And now you are going to die as you should have died before!"

As he spoke he put his hand inside his evening-coat and as he drew it out again something glittered in the moonlight.

Idylla knew what he was about to do, but she could not move, could not cry out.

She was held by the evil which exuded from him, the evil she had felt encroaching upon her night after night until the Marquis had given her the cross to wear.

Caspar Trydell raised his arm.

"Die!"

At that second a voice behind him said authoritatively:

"Stop!"

It was not a shout, it was a word of command that seemed to vibrate through the air and Caspar's instinctive reaction was to turn his head.

He saw advancing towards him the figure of Colonel

Trumble, the High Sheriff from Essex, and from the shrubs on either side of the garden there appeared four Bow Street Runners in their red uniforms.

He looked round in a furtive manner seeking an avenue of escape, only to see the Marquis walking down the steps of the house behind Idylla, a pistol in his hand.

"Sir Caspar Trydell, I charge you with the murder of the Reverend Algernon Salford, Vicar of Gore, and with the attempted murder of your niece, Idylla Trydell. Also of being under suspicion of the murder of her father, John Trydell, your brother!"

The High Sheriff's voice seemed like an indictment of doom and Sir Caspar stared at him wildly.

Then swiftly, so quickly that it was impossible for anyone to stop him, he plunged the long, pointed stiletto which he held in his right hand deeply into his chest.

He staggered and as he fell Idylla felt the Marquis pick her up in his arms.

.   .   .   .

Later when they were alone and Idylla was sipping a glass of wine which the Marquis insisted she should have, she asked:

"Why did . . you not . . tell me?"

"I was so afraid something would go wrong and I should have raised your hopes unnecessarily," the Marquis answered.

"You knew it was . . he who had . . killed Grandfather?"

"I knew, but I needed more proof unless you were to be subjected to a long and searching cross-examination in the Courts. That would have been inevitable if you were the only witness."

"But how did you guess who Papa was?" Idylla enquired.

"I began to think that my friend John might have been your father," the Marquis replied, "when you told me you lived on the other side of the river. John and I used to race each other across that stretch of water when we were young, and if your mother was half as beautiful as you, my darling, I was sure that if he saw her he must have fallen in love."

"Mama was far more beautiful than I could ever be."

"It is impossible for me to believe that," the Marquis smiled.

He kissed her forehead before he went on:

"I wanted to find the proof of their Marriage which would have been in the Register. That was what Caspar was looking for when he ransacked the Vicarage."

"He did that?" Idylla exclaimed in surprise, and the Marquis remembered he had not told her what had occurred.

"Everything will have been tidied away again now," he said comfortingly. "But darling, you will not be going there again."

"But have you proof that Papa and Mama .. were married?" Idylla questioned. "You did not find a record of it in the Register?"

"Because your mother had removed that page and the one which recorded your birth. I have only just learnt that she deposited them both with your Grandfather's solicitor in Chelmsford."

As he spoke the Marquis drew an envelope from his pocket and put it into Idylla's hands.

"If you still doubt me," he said, "and still need proof that you are legitimate, my darling love, here it is!"

Idylla opened the envelope and drew out the two missing pages.

There they were and she could read them for herself!

Her eyes were shining as she looked up at the Marquis.

"Mr. Chiswick brought the letter here this morning," the Marquis explained. "You had gone upstairs to dress for the party, and I did not wish to disturb you. I therefore persuaded him to give me the letter which was addressed to you. It was to be given to you in the event of two things happening."

"What were they?" Idylla asked.

"The first that you should be married," the Marquis said, "the second that you should survive your mother and your Grandfather, which you have done."

"But why? Why did Mama not tell me who my father was?" Idylla enquired.

"Mr. Chiswick explained to me," the Marquis answered, "that your mother told him she had been threatened by a person to whom she would not give a name. There is no doubt in my mind, that it was the threat of death but she was also told that if she spoke of her marriage you would die."

The Marquis's arms tightened as he continued:

"Mr. Chiswick said that when your mother went to see him she was very frightened, but she was brave enough to hand him this letter with the instructions that you were to receive it when you married."

The Marquis smiled.

"And that is what is going to happen, my darling. We will be married as quickly as it can possibly be arranged."

Idylla stared down at the pages of the Register as if

she could hardly believe they were real, then she said:

"Was it because Mama was threatened that made you think Sir Caspar had also killed Papa?"

"Your father had the same injuries on his head as you and your Grandfather," the Marquis replied. "I was convinced it could not be a coincidence. I know now that Caspar Trydell killed his brother, thinking he would then inherit the estates."

The Marquis's voice sharpened as he went on:

"Only when Caspar discovered on Sir Harold's death that everything he possessed had been left first to John, then to any issue John might have, did he realise that you were the rightful heir."

Idylla looked at him in astonishment.

"You .. you mean .. I now own the Trydell Estates?"

"Yes, my darling!" the Marquis said. "But I think you can incorporate them very easily and comfortably with the Estate next door! We will certainly make better provision for your Grandfather's pensioners than Caspar made."

Idylla gave a little inarticulate murmur and hid her face against the Marquis's shoulder.

He took the glass from her hand and set it down on a table and held her very close against him.

"All the unhappiness, the fear and the horror you have been through are over," he said. "The world is a cleaner place now that Caspar Trydell is dead!"

"I need not be .. afraid of anything any .. more," Idylla said, "not even of being a .. witch!"

"Caspar put you on the Druid stones," the Marquis explained, "because he thought you were dead and he wished in some perverted way to defame your corpse and at the same time incite the villagers to further brutality towards witches."

The Marquis felt Idylla tremble and he said:

"We can forget all about it. It is past and done with, except for one thing."

"What is that?" she asked.

"That however many crosses you may wear round your neck, you have, my lovely one, bewitched me!"

He smiled and held her closer still as he said:

"I am under your spell – a spell from which I can never escape and I am convinced will keep me enslaved for the rest of my life."

Idylla lifted her face to his and the Marquis's lips were very close to hers as he said softly:

"You are mine, my darling – mine now and for eternity. My own witch, the only woman I have ever really loved and wanted to marry."

"Are you .. sure of .. that?"

"More sure than I have ever been of anything in my whole life!"

The Marquis paused before he said:

"I knew when I first saw you that you were different from any woman I had ever known and when I kissed you what I felt was so strange, so unaccountable that I could not believe it!"

"It was .. nice?" Idylla asked.

"It was a magic I cannot describe."

He saw the joy in her eyes and went on:

"When you told me, my beautiful one, that you wanted to love me as my mother would have loved me had she lived, I knew I had found what all men seek – the perfect woman!"

"I am not .. perfect .. and I might .. fail you," Idylla murmured.

"You are perfect to me," the Marquis replied, "and I know we will neither of us fail each other."

"That is what I shall .. pray for," Idylla whispered.
"I love you! I love you so completely and absolutely
that I could not live .. without you!"

It was impossible to finish saying the words for the
Marquis's lips, passionate and possessive, were on hers.

They were one, and he knew that, great as was his
need of her as a woman, she was also spiritually a
part of his soul.

The Marquis's kisses grew more insistent, more demanding. He kissed Idylla's eyes, her cheeks, her neck
where a little pulse was beating wildly and then again
her lips.

They were swept away by an ecstasy so tempestuous,
so overwhelming, that it was the power and majesty
of the Divine.

"I love you."

"I .. love .. you."

The words were on their lips, in their hearts and came
from their souls.

Then Idylla felt that the Marquis carried her up into
the starlit Heaven where there was no fear, no evil,
only the perfection of love!

THE UNPREDICTABLE BRIDE

Barbara Cartland

'Give me your daughter in marriage – and I will cancel your debts.'

So wrote the infamous Earl of Meridan to Hester's father, whose rash wagers at the cardtable threatened to lose him his entire estate.

But Hester, already in love and pledged to another man, had a younger sister – the tomboyish Lucinda, whose daring and unconventional behaviour was to cause Lord Meridan more trouble than he had bargained for. . . .

DANCE ON MY HEART

Barbara Cartland

The year is 1929 – and Fiona is alone and penniless in London.
The only job she can find is as a dance hostess at Paglioni's – a
chic and expensive night-club, patronised by the very highest
society people.

It is here that Fiona meets, and falls in love with Jim Mac-
Donald – a man as handsome as he is rich. But it seems that
their passion can never lead to happiness, for Jim is already
committed to another woman, whose dark past and many
secrets bring nothing but unhappiness and the threat of
tragedy . . .

NO DARKNESS FOR LOVE

Barbara Cartland

Walking through a wood on the way back from Castle Combe, Atalanta Lynton encounters a young man sketching. His name, she learns, is Paul – an Impressionist who, like other painters of that school, is reviled and scorned by his countrymen.

Paul and Atalanta fall in love; but she is to go to Paris with her cousin, Viscount Cottersford – who has asked for her hand.

Now Atalanta must choose – wealth and position or love and poverty.

A HEART IS BROKEN

Barbara Cartland

Jilted by Tim, the man she loves, Mela comes to England from Canada to work for her uncle who is a member of the Government. On her arrival, however, she learns that he has been killed in an air raid.

She determines to unravel a mystery regarding her uncle's death and with the help of Peter Flacton – her uncle's political assistant – sets out to bring the truth to light.

During their investigations they find themselves in hopelessly compromising circumstances and to save Peter's reputation Mela marries him – but on her wedding day she meets Tim again . . .